T0086214

Brian Miller Nine Tales
of Dragon Star Terror
(A Non-Novel)

Brian Miller Nine Tales of Dragon Star Terror
(A Non-Novel)

Book Nine

J. Michael Brower

iUniverse books may be ordered through booksellers or by contacting:

iUniverse
1663 Liberty Drive
Bloomington, IN 47403
www.iuniverse.com
844-349-9409

Because of the dynamic nature of the Internet, any web addresses or links contained in
this book may have changed since publication and may no longer be valid. The views
expressed in this work are solely those of the author and do not necessarily reflect the
views of the publisher, and the publisher hereby disclaims any responsibility for them.

Any people depicted in stock imagery provided by Getty Images are models,
and such images are being used for illustrative purposes only.
Certain stock imagery © Getty Images.

ISBN: 978-1-6632-4884-8 (sc)
ISBN: 978-1-6632-4885-5 (e)

Print information available on the last page.

iUniverse rev. date: 12/12/2022

CONTENTS

ACKNOWLEDGEMENT

For the "real" Brian Miller

if it doesn't come bursting out of you
in spite of everything,
don't do it.
unless it comes unasked out of your
heart and your mind and your mouth
and your gut,
don't do it.
if you have to sit for hours
staring at your computer screen
or hunched over your
typewriter
searching for words,
don't do it.
if you're doing it for money or
fame,
don't do it.
if you're doing it because you want
women in your bed,
don't do it.
if you have to sit there and
rewrite it again and again,
don't do it.
if it's hard work just thinking about doing it,
don't do it.
if you're trying to write like somebody
else,
forget about it.

if you have to wait for it to roar out of
you,
then wait patiently.
if it never does roar out of you,
do something else.
if you first have to read it to your wife

or your girlfriend or your boyfriend
or your parents or to anybody at all,
you're not ready.
don't be like so many writers,
don't be like so many thousands of
people who call themselves writers,
don't be dull and boring and
pretentious, don't be consumed with self-
love.
the libraries of the world have
yawned themselves to
sleep
over your kind.
don't add to that.
don't do it.
unless it comes out of
your soul like a rocket,
unless being still would
drive you to madness or
suicide or murder,
don't do it.
unless the sun inside you is
burning your gut,
don't do it.
when it is truly time,
and if you have been chosen,
it will do it by
itself and it will keep on doing it
until you die or it dies in you.
there is no other way.

and there never was.

Charles Bukowski, 1920-1994, *So, You Want To Be a Writer?* from *Sifting Through the Madness for the Word, the Line, the Way*, gratefully acknowledged from the publisher HarperCollins. Research (and much, much respect) for <u>The Donner Party</u>, narrated by David McCullough (1933-2022), and <u>The Dyatlov Pass Incident</u>, by Nick Crowley, very gratefully acknowledged. Cover art: thanks to Bennett Strickler.

Grateful acknowledgment also goes to the songs referenced, Judy Collins, *Judith*; *Something Just Like This*, the Chainsmokers and Coldplay; Karen Carpenter, *Close To You*; Billie Eilish (and her brother Finneas) with *Everything I Wanted*. Also, for *Heavy Metal*, the quote is from the (outstanding, 'speaking' as a teenager, now) movie. <u>Faces of Death</u> quote from Michael Carr, gratefully acknowledged.

ANTI-ZERO

TERRIFIER IN THE MIDDLE KINGDOM

See her how she flies
Golden sails across the sky
Close enough to touch
But careful if you try
Though she looks as warm as gold
The Moon's a harsh mistress
The Moon can be so cold.—Judy Collins, Judith

They make a desert and call it 'peace.'—Tacitus

...more haters than lovers
Slices of doom like taffeta
People are not good to each other
People are not good to each other
One on one
And the beads swing
And the clouds cloud
And the dogs piss upon the roses

And the killer beheads the child
Like taking a bite
Out of an ice cream cone
And the ocean comes in and out
In and out
Under the direction of a senseless Moon
And people are not good to each other.—*Charles Bukowski, The Crunch*

–Good afternoon! It's all very simple, everyone. So let me put it, simply. I, Danillia, *volunteer* myself to go to Asia, China, specifically. I mean, as a one-star-dragon-expeditionary-mission? Just before all companions and dragons leave this Earth? To reconnoiter the Middle Kingdom, as the Lord of the Lizardanians, Littorian, apparently, wishes? I'll make it a colorful visit, that's my watch-word, I'll make it *positively bloom.* Everyone agrees to this—silence means compliance, right? Brian Miller, no one else, if the group pleases, to represent gentle humanity? Even though he's not my companion, don't worry. I won't let him get all 'dragon' on us. I'll defend against his cultural appropriation. No chance on churning my yogurt into KY Jelly, okay my young, vigorous teenager? His "local wives" might like that, but I shan't. However, I'm willing to be this human's step-and-fetch it, ready to go, Brian?

At this extreme insult to <u>me</u> especially, the suggestive, racist stuff was scandalous-alone, I was assured of a negative reaction among the dragon stars. So I looked around, a self-satisfied smirk, my mask.

Shocking, what happen next!

–Sounds reasonable enough for me, right Clareina?

Clare blinked her massive eyes at Larascena.

–Agreeable to you, agreeable to me, too.

Matter concluded, draconianly, as *all* the dragon stars assembled just dismissed it, *entire*. My recent-wives were going to *let* this happen?[1]

Larascena, the great Warlord of *all* Alligatoria, then Clareina, the young Lizardanian, stared at me, with a *'see-ya'* gaze in those myriad (and utterly mysterious), wide eyes. And, thinking nothing, it was all over for them. They began casually looking at the sky, maybe in anticipation of leaving the Earth altogether.

Katrina gazed at me, shaking my arm vigorously.

–Brian Miller, doesn't Danillia <u>hate you</u> most of all? What's this zombie-talk from Clare and Lara? They don't care that you'll be at Danillia's mercy? They think you're going to be okay with her? Not to repeat history, but <u>let's do</u>: Didn't she want the Earth to get destroyed by the Twins of Triton, the twin meteors? Didn't she want Littorian to get strung up, at that ridiculous trial? Didn't she defeat Korillia on Lizardania and then Clare, too, and wanted to make a saurian *shish kabob* out of you? Didn't she also try to—

Danillia grew agitated at the delay in my summons. She snapped her fingers like a shotgun blast busting any double-door-bigly, she was not to be beclowned.

–Hey, hey! The Middle Kingdom awaits, Brian, come here. You deal with that sneaking Russian later, let's go!

At the wonder of all the bagel-mouthed-companions Rachel Dreadnought and Jason Shireman just politely smiled. The leaders of my companion rivals, agreed with Danillia in a delightful way, and actually waived good-bye! Rachel blew me a kiss. It was as if Danillia had a love-affair with me. Jason turned away, *knowing* that

---

[1] Oh, *just now*, one of my kids says, damn Dad, no one understands what in the blue-blazes your even talking about. I said, "Uh"! I covered almost all of it in Book One through Eight! This is written in the French style, hence the exclusion of quotation marks and all. I mean, ever read <u>M/F</u>, by Anthony Burgess, the 1971 novel? This is done just like that. Wasn't Anthony Burgess a "good" writer? So <u>he</u> can do it, but I shan't? That book uses the same style, after-about-one-and-all! Just read along, thesis, antithesis and synthesis, right? <u>This is about two teenagers that try to get reluctant dragon-stars to save the world</u>, and that's all it is! Patience for a Young-Old Man ;-), okay? And let's not read the 'footnotes,' as one Star Dragon says, 'bothersome things!'.

wasn't true. Without another word, leaving all Black World weapons behind (it would be <u>rude</u> to bring those armaments on a supposed peace-mission) Danillia *took me* (and maybe Biblically, too).

On our flight, just when we left Florida, Danillia turned her massive *equine-esque* head around.

–You like flying with me? My little someone-else's companion? Oh, I don't give a country-care whether you're enjoying it or not. Breaking in on your companion-contentment, let's get down to business. I'm sure you *knew* this was coming.

Green, puissant scales rolled by, like I was greased in WD-40. Her vast pinions, upside down now, veined leathery wings, she looked quite majestic. Of a sudden, I felt an extreme grip on my hips. Dragon blood failing fast, I had to think quickly, maybe even abstractly.

–My lady, if you crush my waist together, like I know you certainly can do, I won't be able to—

–Oh, the <u>hole</u> you're digging, and what? Listen for a notable, distinguished *pop*, coming on fast. As I squash your frame into an attractive hood ornament? Wait until my gorgeous muscles make your bones squeeze together like any over-ripe banana. Let's play a game. In about one minute I'll squish all the way through you like an over-ripe grape. Wouldn't that be fun?

–Your pouting abs are the stuff of gods, my lady.

–And your unctuousness is in question, too, right-when I'm about to end you. And once your nature-boy hips are destroyed, we'll get to the business-side of that Evergreen question of the 'rest' of you. I've got a total of ten feet of rock-hard muscle. I mean, just feel those Everest peaks, away up on-my-mightiness!

I was stunned with the power sliding off those giantess biceps. I obligatorily caressed them.

–Wow, they're ultra-hard, my mightiness.

–That's without magic, too, almost sixty-inches across these Cyclopean gigantisms, which will make these human 'hipsters' into solid-bone-cracking-jelly. How many human lifetimes I spent growing my arms, I couldn't tell. Oh, I know, I know. Admittedly, you have *dragon blood* from Larascena, Clareina, and Littorian, right? Maybe more saurians, you're so blessed, Brian. What can't be cured must be endured, but not for long. Thing is, I'm old, very, very old. I have spells for this trip you'll know well. Am I skipping ahead? Not that you could help squealing in your piggy-voice. I'm squishing you like an accordion, crushing right through those star dragon layers of shields running around your bones? Nice resistance, but it's no match for me. How does a guy get so squirted and *ka-smashed* into my dominant arms? How did you get so hopelessly pinched by my angelic seven-inch claws? Human, you reached much too high, and, in the past, I've been wronged too much by little you. Answer to the question *'why'*? My demolishing begins with a spell I've 'hatched' over all the saurians on your 'left side of the bus,' dummy! Don't worry, they'll realize my spell. Realization too late.

I knew I was in the deepest-dragon-borne-trouble. For the tenth time, I couldn't believe <u>my own saurians</u> could be so deceived. They should be watching for a spell from this dragon star. Danillia was, and is, so powerful. Chances *were*, she'd numerous spells saved up.

–Chances *are*, silly human! Chances are! You think straight, pigmy, I'm monitoring you.

I did have my mental defenses up, but up against Danillia? She'd invaded some of my thoughts, too. Maybe she couldn't follow along completely? I had to take a risk on that. The dragon star was a daughter of God? Definitely of a <u>fallen</u> god.

–Danillia, I have to say your muscles are feminine and structurally ginormous, too.

–Dispense with your obsequiousness when life's dangerously close to ending. Your mind's blown-in a bit now, eh? Vitals, when at attention, constitute a form of muscle, right, Brian? At some point, you have to get more strategic with your (dragon-star-induced) apparatus. Oh, I know your old human debate, is it a muscle or an organ? Magnificent, Olympian phallus? Guess what? I've a mega-muscle, *too*, and can griddle that mega-lance down to mere mush-and-slush. Even if it reaches three feet, enticed with its veiny goodness, as my two un-favorite saurians like? Unlike Clare and Lara, you'll not violate me. If you *just* do, there on my back, I'll squeeze, shift-snuff, and eviscerate that brawny shaft into mincemeat, to sludge, with my virginial galaxy-box. It will be mega-death of your meat-hammer, grinding your mighty bazooka into a soft, moist paste. Like the sound of that? Some of your people, our pets, *sure* do. Your "favorite" muscle ground-dog-down to nothing but gunk-goo? I'm getting dragon-star-moist just thinking about destroying your shifty-shaft. Mashing, mushing, rutting and ploughing your miserably weak body, Lilith-on-top, right? I'll turn your proud Puff-the-One-Eyed-Dragon into a spineless slush, like ten-day-gone-yogurt, dripping to the floor? I will close my viral muscle completely around your stunned-muzzle-angler, obliterating that trembling invader, until you are literally mega-*priss*-throttled. I'll *mortify your pride*, oh, yes. Then I'll eunuchize you; ripping all your blood-soaked-bowling-ball-sized-gonads up and out with my unyielding, saurian-superwoman-ripping-claws. Ken-Doll-Here-You-Cum, right? Can't you just see my shiny teeth chumping on those veiny-jewels for my *Elevenses*, you gutter snip Clydesdale-dead-stallion?

I swallowed, gamely enough, at this sinister and scatological monologue.

—And then—alas! I can't tell you of The Donner Party, a shame it'd be if you missed out on that, my lady!

The crushing-squeezing was stilled.

—The Donner Party, what's that, speak!

I went on pleadingly, if not with any particular pleasantry.

—Just a story, but oh, what a story it is, too bad you'll miss.

—Stupid street cleaner of the human shit-conscience, maybe I'll get a goat to lick your vitals, right? Now doff your hat, we're leaving Florida, at 5,000 feet up? I'm just thinking about licking your selected dragon minges, don't mind me. What god would goddamn want you to 'transcend' anywhere? You vile creature, as

I'll show you, anon. Now we are flying over Mississippi. I've slowed down this dragon-flight, I don't want <u>to miss</u> this, my near-to-death human! Good that you have an atmosphere, an 'environment,' that I'm providing, no less, but I need to hear your servile voice. Oh, I just need to *know* this story, I'm just strangely frenzied about it. I see you've protected your mind, I could get the memory out by ripping it from your brain. You've drunk (or drank?) dragon-star blood, and a lot of it, too, so even I am subject to Universalian language to be your servile student. I don't want to miss this story, if you've got a good one?

–Danillia my story is just the greatest event of human suffering that you could imagine, my regal lady, taking place out West. And it's not just the greatest event of human anguish, it's distress in general of all kinds, even a dragon would want to know, can you relax your mighty grip so I can tell it, my lady? But it's okay to finish me, I—

–Let me hear <u>first</u> of the Donner Party, speak Brian and I might let you survive a little longer, only in order to tell me. So speak!

–My lady, so please you. In the 1840s, folks needed to get to California so—

–California? Oh, that's one of your nuisance states, I guess? It doesn't matter from up here in the air, states are just an artificial construction. I can identify them, because, well, I'm a dragon star, duh! We'll fly over California soon, just give me the location?

–I've seen maps, I can't give you just where it is, my lady so—

–It's something to go on, think it to me, maggot-minion?

I cringed at that abysmal-reference (she had a habit of that), but I dutifully obeyed the dragon star. I didn't want to rub her scales the wrong way unless surrounded by saurian friends. At this point, I had no friends, at least, near me. Flying with her, a harsh mistress, tell a *good* story, or <u>splat</u>, overfilled trash bag would be my end (with squashed hips).

–Hmmm, what's this, thought defenses up? I could penetrate

those notions, even if they are saurian-based. You've no real experience with a mind as old as mine.

–That'd give me a headache, interfering with my story, so—

–Oh, alright, tell on. Tell, tell!

–At this time, 1846 was the worst winter on record, my esteemed lady. Only 20,000 or so immigrants lived west of the Mississippi River. Then it developed into a human-flood, as more people wanted to move West, for various reasons. High in the Sierra-Nevada, there was the tale of the sad Donner Party. Ambition, greed, stupid failures, and, all-the-while, wanting to take a short-cut. In 1845, an author wanted to get more folks to go West. That writer was Lansford W. Hastings. So he wrote the *Immigrants Guide to Oregon and California*, wishing people to move West.

–Why's that, my human? Be quick!

–Financial panic, outbreaks of sickness and that insatiable need for *Manifest Destiny*, to move West. For instance, the Mormons moved to Utah with Brigham Young—

–Alright, go on, speed it up!

–Yes, my queen. Hastings had never really seen the route he thought would be best. For some, the American Dream was a tragedy of the worst kind. In April 1846, a bunch of wagons started out from Springfield, Illinois, George and Jacob Donner and James Reed, took their families West. Reed was leading the group at first, but he acted like royalty, you see. Doesn't that sound familiar? Woops, strike that. They had a big wagon with a stove, cots for sleeping, spring-cushioned seats, the *Pioneer Palace Car*. It was an elaborate affair too, my eminence. Independence, Missouri was where they were headed to get into that 'long wagon train,' going to California and Oregon. They had to go next to Indian Territory, so that—

–You mean Native Americans, right?

–Well, uh, they were called 'Indians' because the original discoverers, from Portugal or Spain, were on their way to India, and just never changed it back, I guess. That's an example of a *sobriquet*, my lady.

–What fruit-loops those explores were; just go on.

–Ah, sure, my queenly. It was a journey full of perils, and, did you know, about 50% of the people on the Donner Party were under 18? It was an epic and epical, that's for sure, 2,500 miles until they could get to Sutter's Fort, in California. They couldn't pass over such a distance like a winged saurian can. Wind-swept plains, three or four mountain ranges, half a dozen scorching deserts, and time was everything. They had to get over the Sierra-Nevada mountains before snow came. Hasting's Cutoff assured them they'd make it. Hasting's pamphlet tantalized the Donners and the Reeds. They thought they could go over the Wasatch Mountains, under the Great Salt Lake, through the desert and through the Rubies, into California. They started out in the company of 7,000 wagons, at least that's what Tamsen Donner said. The wagons started on May 12th. However, the Mexican-American War of 1846 was just beginning, and everyone was going to that—maybe, at some point, I'll tell you of the story of the Alamo, but that was 1836. Anyhow, they got to the Big Blue River—

–Yup, and there it is, Kansas, see my simian?

–Oh, yes, my queen. I'll prefer it if you don't *refer* to me as—

–And you're in no position to make preferences, scat-monkey. Go on with the story before I turn you inside out. Don't think I can't: I'll drive my hand into your mouth and pull you out by the ass-sphincter.

I swallowed a sickly stick of massive cancer.

–The *Pioneer Palace Car* was a labor to them. Margaret Reed's mother was the first casualty. She died of consumption.

–What's that, quickly?

–It's TB.

–You and your abbreviations. I'll kill you for that, just not right now. What's TB?

–Tuberculosis. My lady.

–And that is?

–Plague, an obscenity, it'll kill you.

–You mean it will kill <u>*you*</u>, simple mandrill!

–Not me, your highness, at least, not now.

–Oh, yes, of course, of course. The Tree of Life, <u>bestial</u> that it's *in* you. No real matter. I'll have my revenge on certain dragons for that one. You can still die by violence, but I'm getting ahead of myself. Go on!

–On June 27th, my saurian pre-eminence, they reached Fort Laramie. They were only a week behind schedule. At this point, an old friend they saw at the fort tried to convince Mr. Reed to follow the regular route. He was sure wagons couldn't go over Hasting's Cutoff. Just the need to take a short-cut in life, we are all going to die one day, so—

–That is, *you are*, ape-teenager.

Danillia's knowing glance, as she shifted a massive eye back and up to me, with a self-same serpentine smile.

–…you have to go for it, sometimes. If your human, you have to. Reed was a good guy, reasonable. You have to take a short-cut, if you're sure of it. So on July 20th, they reached the Little Sandy River. Most people chose right, but the Donner's selected the left road. They elected a captain, and Reed's imperial ways and wealth had rubbed people the wrong way. They elected George Donner. Just another mistake in democracy, right there. A week later, they rolled into Fort Bridger, with Jim Bridger running it like a trading-post. Mr. Hastings, the author they were effectively following, wasn't there, he'd went on ahead, with other wagons, saying any other immigrants could follow behind. Hastings Cut-Off was a saving of 350 or 400 miles. According to Mr. Hastings, that is. But Mr. Bridger said it was a good way to go. Captain Sutter's Fort was only 700 miles away, seven weeks, so said James Reed. But they were stimmed—

–What the *hell* does that word mean? You alphabet-mafia-Zulu, it doesn't translate to Universalian at all, talk in plain language or I'll throttle you, raggedy-chimp!

I was 5,000 feet up on a hostile dragon star, I had to watch myself.

–Sorry, my lady: That means they came to a halt. The road ahead was not good. It was already early in August. They stopped at Echo Canyon in Utah and—

–You mean right there, maggoty-ass-chimpanzee?

This saurian had the eyes of a three-or-four times eagle and the GPS of a, well, a dragon!

–Yes, lady, there. Wow, you are making progress to the Middle Kingdom, a place I'd like to see, so please you. So Hastings, in a written note they found on the road, said to stay there to find a better way. James Reed went to find him. Hastings was reluctant to lead the immigrants and so Reed had to do the job of leading people up Big Mountain. Then they reached to shore of the Great Salt Lake, it'd taken longer than they thought. On August 27th, the 87 immigrants had 600 miles to go. West and then south. Summer was going fast. They had to cross the desert, the Salt Desert. It was August 30th. The oxen bolted, when they went across the desert, and it was a disaster. Five days to cross the desert, 36 oxen where lost, and the *Pioneer Palace Car* was abandoned.

–Damn. They are having a hard time of it.

This was the first sign of sympathy and I longed to hear this. Then she followed with this zinger.

–…right, you yard ape?

–Very hard time, my highness. They could not get back to Fort Bridger. Inventory of provisions was drawn up. They didn't have enough to make it to California. On September 27th they reached the Humboldt River, in Nevada where the trail met up with the established one. Could they make it before the snow fell? The race was on. Hasting's Cut-Off was 125 miles longer and most-everything was lost going through it, including a lot of animals. On October 5th, Reed got it real trouble…

–What happened, *say it* orangutan, or I'm going to beat your ass from inside your mouth! And don't think I <u>can't</u> do it, either. Let me interrupt you with this little thought. Isn't the conditioning of Artificial Intelligence the end of humanity? Nuclear war looms, just as the Military-Industrial complex desires. We have our companions and just want to go, the hell with human affairs. But you, Brian Miller, keep thinking of <u>excuses</u> causing us to stay, causing <u>me</u> to disobey. I want to go, you keep me here. So, I've got to play, my way, the dragon-borne mode. I'll show you where your excuses can take you!

I forced myself to go on. Backtalk here, a huge splat down on the rocks below. Or some kinda unknown ass-whipping.

–My lady, if I can go on with my story, he killed somebody (like *I'd* like to do). Reed was trying to get this other guy after he thrashed his oxen, and the guy turned right-around and started flogging Reed with his whip! Reed got his hunting knife and killed this dude. People wanted Reed hung but settled on exile. Reed rode out of camp, banished, and his family cried endlessly. I guess the 'democratic' decision was made, maybe we can chat about that but not right now. The Donner party traveled on. The immigrants knew they were coming apart. On October 12th, Piute Indians killed a portion of oxen with poisoned arrows. Now they were down below 100 head of cattle. They reached the Truckee Lake. On October 19th, food was nearly gone—they were desperate.

At this point, an actual shiver made itself felt on me. Maybe it was from the dragon? A chance-thought occurred.

We are getting somewhere, I knew she couldn't be that cruel, maybe she is coming around to sympathize with these settlers, you are doing right with this story, I just knew it!

–Then good news—the men they'd sent on to Sutter's Fort returned with seven mules loaded with food. They were going to make it after all!

–Geez, I thought there was something to this story, good that they are going to make it over that last peak. 'Course, I could grab a big piece of land and then fly them over the mountain. Or just turn into an attractive Godzilla and step over that facial scab, sprinkling the Donner's down at Fort Sutter!

–It didn't work out that way, my lady, because they rested at Truckee Lake for five days—and then, winter storms took over. Thing is, they shouldn't have waited so long. Before that, the Donner's wagon wheel broke and George Donner cut his hand, trying to fix it. That delayed the party further. George's hand turned into gangrene. Meantime, the way out was blocked by snow. The blizzard did its job, and the pass out of Truckee Lake was completely blocked. They'd lost time by literally a day or two, to get over the pass, so they had to build a winter camp. And it snowed, and snowed and yes, you guessed it. The folks at Sutter's Fort, had to save the immigrants. Reed was in charge of relief parties, he'd made it through to California. But he could get no men to do it; they were all off fighting the Mexicans. The people tried to get out. They couldn't. The 81 members of the Donner Party consisted of 25 men, 15 women, and 41 children in two winter camps. And all that you do, Danillia, can't compare with starvation. And then what follows is...

–Is what, my little baboon?

–It's cannibalism, my lady.

The saurian was silent.

–So? On with it!

–So say that _word_, my highness, then, I'll go on.

The reptilian looked around, surprised. In pleasant flight, with an atmosphere around this me, she <u>had</u> to say it. The saurian had to *plead* with me to continue.

–Okay my temporarily privileged human. _Please_?

–Alright my eminence. Most of cattle were killed, the Donners had to stay until next Spring. The people were miserable, all starving. Thanksgiving came. The snow, about three-feet-deep. It continued to accumulate, foot-on-foot. All cattle killed and consumed. Bark, leaves, old bones, anything to eat during these dark days. On December 16th, the strongest ones, called themselves "The Forlorn Hope," tried to escape. Snow blindness hit the selected settlers as they walked high in the California Mountains, hopelessly lost. Cannibalism soon took over the "Hope." God was asked to help. He…wasn't available. Someone died, and then another and another. Someone cut the meat off the dead, one Patrick Dolan. The awful food revived them, so they struggled on. The two Indians, from Sutter's Fort, were killed, then eaten. At Truckee Lake, people were dying left and right. Someone had to help these people: Relief parties were send. Assistance had to come. James Reed led the second relief party. The first party was on its way. Meanwhile, people were buried in the snow, with blankets over them. That is, those who weren't on the plate for others to eat. On February 19th, the first relief party was on the frozen Truckee Lake. No one was there. Then, a woman emerged from a hole in the snow. "Are you men from California… or do you come from Heaven?" The relief party could only take 24 of the people out. Then, on February 26th—

–Hey, why didn't someone fish at the lake?

–What?

–Manners, mind, beast-of-the-field. Never-you-mind. Why didn't they fish, wanna-be-reptile?

–Well, you're right. Uh, I don't know, maybe they did, and it was unsuccessful, my lady. It's a good question.

–Go on, man-ape.

That really grated on me. However, I knew the destructive power of the beast, me trying to subtly correct this sickening set of pejoratives.

–The Donner Party's troubles were far from over. Four more relief parties struggled to get the Donner Party from the high snow. The scenes enacted in those months can never be forgotten, tales of aguish, sorrow of mothers before dissolving children, the men no food to bring home. When the first relief party reached the Lake, Patty Reed, then eight years old, wanted to stay behind to care for her brother, Thomas. "Well, ma, if you never see me again, do the best that you can." Then the second relief party came to help the first. James Reed was leading it. Margaret Reed hadn't seen James in all that time, five months. At the Lake, it was all chaos. People went crazy, just crazy. Maybe you'd know what that's like? Demons, not humans, lingered at the Truckee, and even the Native Americans avoided the immigrants when they witnessed cannibalism.

George Donner and Tamsin Donner were inseparable. They died and were cannibalized. It was all a horror show. The fourth relief party was delayed by a month. On April 21st, the fourth relief team left the lake and on April 25th, they reached Bear Valley. All of the survivors had come out of the mountains. It could have been avoided if people hadn't gone for a 'short-cut'. That's how it was for the Russian Revolution, too. Lenin and Trotsky wanted all the Russians to 'jump ahead,' to defy their DNA, live socialism and communism. Thing was: The peasants; just 'little' bourgeoisie waiting-to-happen. It wasn't to be, and they got Stalin, instead. Millions died as a result. I think the <u>clothes</u> people wore, the uniforms, de-humanized people, let them kill their fellow creatures. Well, that's all I've to say on this. People keep making different choices, but all the mistakes are repeated (over and over). Maybe that could change on different worlds, like in the Goldilocks Zone or the Butterfly Zone, this, the Donner Party and the Russian Revolution was the Twilight Zone. For me, I've try to 'get ahead' and have dragons here to lead us all to a better life. I think my time with you will be that result and that's what I get, trying, sincerely, to make things better. I've made them worse, that is, this flight with you. Humans can be animals and your comparing me with lower forms of life, isn't really wrong. We <u>are</u> animals. For the Donner Party, 87 people started out. 46 survived. 41 died. 5 women, 14 children and 22 men, dead. Two-thirds of the men buried (if not cannibalized). The family of the Donners suffered most. Now, the Donner Camp is a tourist attraction. A real shame, and only a true-teenager can tell this story sincerely to a saurian. People are fragile, please know that if nothing else. The thing we have is love, the Reed's love shown in the Sierra-Nevada mountains when James found some of his family, two children still remained at Truckee Lake. I will tell you this, my noble reptilian, as a reminder to all: "Remember, never take no cut-offs and hurry along as fast as you can." That's from Virginia Reed. When the human race, when people like Virginia stop fighting against the odds, against the frigid cold—and even fighting a crazy saurian like you—that's when we lose our humanity. And that's a good place to end such a story, my lady.

When the Donner story was over, I reacted with a smidgen of hope over the malicious intentions of Danillia. The saurian was indeed hesitant. At least, I thought.

–Wow, that was a good story. Your execution is temporarily halted, the Pacific Ocean is just there. I do like your spark, Brian, even if you are notoriously misdirected. Can you see the ocean, from here? Maybe only I can. I've an idea, let's play a little game. Back to the scene of the crime? Ah, <u>this</u> is just the time for it.

I was confused, but that didn't matter to Danillia. The winged saurian warped down to the Nevada-California mountains, arriving at this sign:

Donner Camp
PICNIC GROUND
Historical Site
Tahoe National Forest

–Well, see how 'picnic ground' is in larger letters? That's wormwood for me. Just let me at those '*tourons*,' if we should find any. Bad day for them if we do. And stop your confounded, faux-melancholic face, Brian, or I'll squish and squashed it off. And you know I can. So, Brian. Know what I've been doing, of late?

–No, my queen, please inform me?

–Why, <u>killing humans</u>, of course! What do you think Jason Shireman was up to, just my arm candy?

I was in profound shock.

–Ah, your legs are shaking. Don't shake too much, someone will get ideas, you little two (or three?) timer. I'll keep you from smashing yourself in the vitals, believe me.

With an iron will, I relaxed my legs.

–A selection of your people have written in, or contacted me on Twitter, Facebook, Snapchat, TikTok, all that social media stuff, asking me, underline particularly me, Danillia, to end them. Must have heard (or read) of my superpowers-superpower over every other dragon star, this happens anywhere I go. Everything and anything is just hook-ups and contacts, anyway! Jason coordinated it all, as a good companion should.

–Is that so, my lady?

At first, I didn't believe her.

–Don't frenchtoast me. Anyone and everyone would be graced to have a god like *moi* finish them, end them. Hell, had to do something when you delayed dragon stars all that time? Jason Shireman understood. He even endorsed it. Oh, I admit, most are sick and old or just 'sick' literally. I've had 54 humans, so far. Some quickly, some longer. I'm very good with human bodies, too. Most are men. They are tired of this life and want, *need,* a dragon to obliterate them utterly. Star dragons are an imposing 'ender' don't you think? And there have been a few young ones. I've had a few women, too, very young females, the kind wanting to die in my powerful claws. And a treat to me, some were pregnant! Hideous you say? Know why? Because they couldn't take their *givens* in this world. A couple of examples: A middle age man at 56? I destroyed that one, proud to do so. Dragon have to make sacrifices for our pets. First, I allowed him his jollies, you know, lifting him up and down, grabbing his vitals and jerking him off, just stuff like that. Men are all about sex and power, they have no other redoubt! Then, repeatedly and rapidly bored, I ripped an electric shock to his face, knocking his eyes out, which hung there just like red cords, sorta like mini-belt hooks? That was fascinating to me, for about eight seconds, then human-driven-generation-Z-boredom-kicked-in. Damn, I've been around humans too long. So he started screaming. I zipped his mouth closed, I've a spell for that, thank goodness. Nuisance <u>screaming</u> indeed. I admit, being a Lizardanian, I'm not 'magically made,' not like an Alligatorian. Crocs have fire, so hot no human can imagine it, that's their gift. The Wysterians, well, they know magic and everything dragon-associated. Me? I hate, can't *stand*, human screaming. Then I stripped him buck-naked, ripped his nails off (all 20 of them), broke his arms, legs and femur, burned his now flaccid off, put my claws through his intestines, stirring them up like so much crimson lasagna, shattered a glass and forced it down his throat, then I burned him *entire* without impacting the nerves, a very skilled thing, requiring a real intimacy with human bodies. Then I just finished him with a little dragon magic—<u>*trigeminal neuralgia*</u> lasting as long as I felt. I didn't let him go unconscious, disallowing those pain-killers like endorphins and serotonins and stuff. Oh, no. I wasn't giving him anything, inflicting the worst pain I could produce. I pride myself on the level of suffering I can cause. For the rest, I just went through my medical book on all the worse pains you humans can feel. Then—

–My goodly lady, I think I've heard enough.

–I'll decide what is <u>enough</u>, simian-silly. Roasting women in a bronze bull is perhaps my favorite torture. Did that on one grimy, foul, raggedy young bitch. Made her nose into a bone-crushed-triangle, too. Then, I smashed her brain-in, so slowly, with my left hand, called it my "Neurocranium Crush," wish you'd seen it. With that move, I'm able to force the brain out of her mouth. And the tongue goes first, see? I've distended her jaw, Cobra-like, easy work for *Moi*. Yes, I do magic with some victims: Numerous stonefish stings, gallstones, tetanus, rusty nails inserted just anywhere, multiple appendix bursts, intense gout, flaying skin, dislocations (I'm very good at that!), massive kidney stones that are just intolerable (for my men, mainly, like giving birth times 100), testicular torsion cord twists, and slow-motion-ripping of bones is my excruciating thing to do with these God-(god?)-given claws. And, my child, I'm going to do the same to you!

The star dragon marshalled her brutal fists together, cracking them mightily, a truly unfathomable force. And sure enough, at Truckee Lake, around the Donner's camp, five families were touring. I took a little risk.

Run, run, run!

The reptilian was positively giggling at the tourists nosing-around. Then she reacted to my contemplation, alert as any thought-Tom-cat.

Don't, sucker! I'll spread and slit your buttocks open like a <u>sea bass</u> in front of all these tourons. Better pucker up, don't want any of those innards displayed? That fillet is <u>easy</u> for those who know. My 'environment' will just direct your notions to me, anyway, so sit by your goddamn dish. See, human, even your thoughts are known to me. Neither your body nor your feelings can escape my saurian clutches. Clutches! Oh, I enjoyed that final word, love to say it, good that you've given me an incident to 'wrap it' around. Like the pun? Oh, let me enjoy!

I discontinued thinking in their direction immediately. I was completely downcast, because this dragon was certifiably crazy. Danillia needed a mad house, definitely so. I'd never would go with her, knowing the extent of her sinister phantasms.

Every/anything the dragon did, in her own mind, was justified.

She wasn't sympathetic or concerned in the least for human-kind. The saurian was like any human world-leader: hungry for individual ambition, to make world-history <u>her</u> way. Anyone getting in the way, would just have to be eliminated. That did not include selected humans, Danillia's companion for instance, and a few, fortunate others. The Lizardanian had the magic-power, inducing the world-over, to get what she wanted. That, no matter what.

The dragon star landed with a vigorous flourish, melting her wings inside herself. I, her faux-companion, hopped off. The drop was four or five feet, but I was used to it, dragon-blood notwithstanding.

She gathered the group together, like a Pied-Piper-of-Ham-Bloody-Burglar-Hill. All five families came together, crowding around her, all with admiration for the great beast. The dragon star smiled sweetly, not revealing any sign of her myriad teeth. The reptilian waved her hands at them, even hugging the parents, making them feel at ease. The elders just dismissed me. She nodded at her extreme bulk, bulwarking strongly for each and every tourist, feeding their eyes like a Donner Camp victim of famine. Of course, mesmerism took them all. I forgave them of at least that. First time in front of a dragon (star)? No doubt. And no one even thought to signal anyone with cellphones, or some such. Why would they when Danillia's subtle manipulation washed over the tourists-complete? Didn't they want a 'selfie' with the dragon? Even that was tertiary in their thoughts. A shame and a sham notion, Danillia's magic would prevent any phones from operating, anyway. That might interfere with any ghoulishness, which would follow, anon.

Danillia lifted, with both mini-Godzilla hands, picking up two gigantic boulders with ease, these weighing in excess of twenty tons. These rocks tightened her body, as was her wont. I was accustomed to such power-displays. Still, all the tourists whispered at this, like *teetering* to a Wilhelm scream. She nestled down, amazing tail making a scaled ring, that the children could climb up. She rocked the giant boulders, in slow motion, up and down for hungry, venerating eyes to see.

Yes, and sit they did, tantalized at fondling the saurians' massive, stunningly oblique sinews. I, mouth parted, stood back, almost *forced* back. I was part of her scheme, too.

With her great reptilian head, she had the kids come up and literally caress her Cyclopean biceps. With a magical entreaty, Danillia made the peaks stand at ridged attention, sculpted, way-up-on-majesty. Frankly, I'd never seen such a pouting structure on any saurian woman's biceps, reaching Everest heights. The youths, thinking they were in heaven and an angel was sat before them, they reached up, willingly, fondling the vastness of the saurian's mighty arms. With the adolescents, all thrown around into a make-shift corral of her tail, the parents hung off to the left, albeit, joyfully entertained. To emulate the children, feeling-away at her colossal saurian body, affected (and positively *infected*) the parents in the most peculiar way.

Tremors of delight ran through all eight children. They were dazzled, properly aligned on Danillia's sinuous tail. Maybe she had a spell on them.

<u>Probably</u> she didn't.

So right up under the sign, SITE OF THE BREEN CAMP, Donner Party, 1846-7, the saurian acted out. And what a horrendous performance, suitable for a saurian-at-war-with-all-humankind (only, these humans didn't know it).

Nevertheless-and-all-the-more, the children cossetted, caressed and playfully touched the dragon star's cobble-stone-abs, giggling. They wondered at the tremors spouting and sprouting-out of those impressive scales, making Danillia's mega-ton-obliques into rippling planks of green, strengthened steel.

–Yes, I'll abase myself so you can get both hands around my peaks on this ginormous bicep. Come, come, get your kiddy-passions out. Those boulders are a minuscule twenty tons apiece, appropriate enough for you? I knew you human kiddies would like this little strength display. You five boys, goodness what's going on in your loins, right? Your, what, 11 or 12 years old? Three girls and five boys? That's pleasant as all get-out. Think of me as your gender slave, I'll do whatever you wish, immediately?

Not following exactly, the children when along with the dragon-hymn of Danillia, rejoicing. If you weren't *used to it*, however, as I was. At this point, Danillia was on the verge of orgiastic victory over her new-found-minions. Cuddling and encouraging them on her massive tail. That elongated structure Danillia held absolutely still. Like rats on random meat, they singularly and collectively "felt the reptilian up" into crowning majesty, she bending obediently down.

This is what humans, even young ones, must do for a dragon, oh, the shear naivety of it all. Be completely mystified, by me and mine. What a terrifier <u>I'm</u> going to give them, and you, Brian Miller Human, like John in Revelation, here to see all!

The terrific things, the mass-Hobbesian-horrifiers, this creature <u>did</u> to the eight innocent broods, no one has any words for. It was unbelievable, ineffable, unnamable, unimageable. I won't go all-H.P. Lovecraft on you, I've an <u>obligation</u> to describe, at least some of it, the rest, Upchuck Metropolis, choking to death on my own sick.

Of a sudden, Danillia brought the two massive rocks together, tons and tons of raw-unexpurgated-muscle-power. Spitting and splitting through flesh and bones, right on the upper-bodies and heads, of all the unknowing kids. A sheen of blood spouted from each of them; two eyes, four, no six, arrived at my feet, dancing around like coins at any Penny Arcade machine. The horrible, surprised orbs looked up at me.

Snake eyes?

Maybe a spell caused by Danillia.

<u>Probably</u> that. Their faces were splatted on the 'environment,' around me, filaments and fragments of a once-human design. At least the atmosphere was still up, but it had all the kid's skin sliding and slipping down like oiled-film on a rainy day. Those observers had astonishment and fear build into their very flesh with the combined, reddened offal. My eyes, windshield wipers, crying. The 'environment' acting like a cerise window of absolute horror, the children looking more like bloody insect-window-splats on a speeding car.

You remember when someone said, 'you are the monster here'? I've seen it wandering around in your thoughts like a pinball. Now, it's me, <u>me</u>, ME, I'm the monster, and little you? Just my lickspittle. Isn't that better <u>than</u> minion, you pre-food?

A miscellaneous child was spilt slowly open in the serpents' mega-hands. For the other children, it ended quite quickly. Two others, it was minutes to the end, but *what* insane minutes!

Danillia ruined all of them, but that wasn't the end of their trouble at her sudden arrival. Death be not proud? The star dragon would make it <u>proud</u>, the red delights and multiple sorrows, the ultra-demise-dealer.

At-the-sudden, chaos-and-dispensed cruelty, Danillia laughed (and thought) down to me.

You like this? This was mere foreplay! I've the godlike strength to perform boiling, keelhauling, Catherine wheels, extracting brains with crushing hand power, pears of anguish (with my claws alone, I can stretch out anyone's mouth or down-backside-south), Diogenes' Pants, Judas Cradles, Blood Eagles and a speeded-up version of Scaphism.

The saurian turned to the frightened adults.

–Given I've something planned for Brian, we'll just have to go with something quick for you guys, right?

Only one woman was pregnant. I lamented it (so fully), praying Danillia wouldn't notice her. Danillia suddenly turned to me and smiled all those seven-inch teeth.

–Let's have some fun—heard of Roe vs. Wade?

With a profound effort, I responded.

–My lady, I'm familiar.

–Not as familiar as this god-serpent, watch this. Sploot yourself right there, or I'll teeth-strafe you!

In a flash, the dragon star appeared in front of the pregnant woman.

–Well. Good afternoon! Like what I did with those brats? Care for a little pick-me-up?

She muscularly lifted the woman. That was around the neck, to negate the nuisance screaming. With the right arm, she made an appalling "T" like any expert, but sinister, coroner. The sight was more than any sane human could stand, as entrails, ice-cream scooped, running with a sticky, slimy squirt, spilled (bloody) everywhere. A single seven-inch claw made a dark cherry wine universal. Then, Danillia bit her head off, like any guillotine, all incisors and fangs.

I couldn't believe this was happening. Then I thought to my star dragons. The 'environment' prevented me from communicating with anyone, even my weapons and Kerok-given pistols. Danillia was very thorough, and *would be*, all the hapless humans her result.

–*Ta-da.* Oh, don't worry, about the others who ran, I'll just draw-and-quarter them. Thinking to my other saurian friends about my mankind-escapades? I'm sure your 'environmentally dealt with,' true? They can't escape me. <u>You</u> can't escape me. Nothing can. So, therefore, arrest me, Brian, I'm convicted of ultra-carnal fierceness, put the cuffs on me, for just this!

Laughing like any insane person, the strapping reptilian gripped the pregnant woman by her arms, lifting the gurgling lady. My jaw hit the grass, almost literally. Then the Lizardanian ripped the baby from the womb, opening the bulbous stomach with her tail. At that instance, the reptilian almost lost control of the little babe, slipping on the misplaced placenta. I stole a furtive look, seeing an infant girl, squirming into the afternoon sunlight.

–Come here you little battery-powered ballerina, wanna see what's inside a saurian?

The reptilian dropped the decapitated female and ate the infant, mercifully whole. Before she <u>did</u> eat it, Danillia stripped all the skin off the suckling in about two or three seconds. I was appalled to hear the tot <u>not</u> scream at being so graphically skinless, but *howl* like a benighted wolf cub. The star dragon then chewed on the ambilocal cord, just for a carnal dessert.

–My goodness, it's just like eating spaghetti, only tastier, too! Much better than the other three. Did you know my otherwise insatiable appetite is <u>increased</u> with all this violence, and all this killing of human flesh? Oh, it's just the Velociraptor in me, can't get away from my DNA, my outrageous muscles, giantess teeth, arms that could crush the Empire State Building to shreds, my talons are mega-spears, oh, its gross-out-gorgeous, right Brian?

–The other three?

–You see, simian, a couple of the 54 were pregnant. One didn't even know it. I corrected her! And when she <u>knew</u> she'd killed another human presenting herself before me, I...corrected *them both*. I felt like a Vermont school-teacher, remember those times, my monkey-boy? Did that baby squirm like a slimy salmon! And if I can get closer to God, (if there is *any*) by eating human brains, Brian, well, why not?

Quick as any wink, the two adults hunted down, crunched to the dirt before me by magic alone. The suffering on their faces was obscured by my tears. I was crying now, couldn't help them.

Increasing her size slightly, another surprise was in order. The dragon star mounted the first flabbergasted human like copulation was going to occur.

–Oh, don't worry Brian. My companion human can give me satisfaction, be assured of that. Set your picadilloes down, you ludicrous-kid. This creature is just—in my way. What spirit does my little human pet possess? Let's just see, lemme see some soul!

Both human legs had talons run through them. That delighted Danillia. Then, the screaming started. *Not* to my monster-mini-dinosaur's liking. She squashed every head like a water-filled balloon. Then she literally ripped-up the now-silent animals, with a disgusting squishing making me want to hurl.

Danillia drew her legs and fingers back and out, splitting the corpse's appendages with a loud rip. The brain, however, had been hammered in advance, just another shredded crimson-sponge.

–Tattered and threadbare for humans is a saurian-right, *right* Brian? I'll get the other parent with a regular draw-and-quartering, not even the mightiest Clydesdale will have anything on me, I'll show you the way to properly engage the brain and the spinal cord to register the extreme amount of worldly pain. Oh, shoot, the brain's already kicked-off. Too bad. How do you feel, when I kill, Brian, makes you want to yak, right? Is this saurian acting without God, really defying Him? You humans kill 600 rabbits a day at some gang-banging-in-her-stomach-slaughterhouses? Bunny paws sold as good-luck charms? God knows how many cows, pigs, chickens, and whatever you guys kill? And you lament at my killing some worthless, backwards kids-n-parents? I could have arm-squished all these shit-brats to death, breaking their stupid necks, but I had mercy, right? I smashed almost all of them with these boulders. Isn't that mercy enough? Those twin-asteroids, the Twins of Triton, were large enough to just finish everyone off in a mere whim! And you and that Russian girl (at least, a <u>piece</u> of her) prevented it from happening. Well! I'll give you back all you lost. Does existence have any meaning at all? I'll give my answer. It's *narcissistic discompassion* of all mankind (with some exceptions). Throw up now, I command it.

At this point, I was up-chucking this morning's breakfast. Danillia seemed triumphant, watching me yak, down on ground, as any animal.

–You think about these children, that my torturing, agonizing a little kid can hinder me, a dragon star? Obviously, you don't understand the <u>alien</u> life of me. Metalaw overthrown? I thought Clare and Lara could teach you at least that. You have your Metalaw out there, somewhere? It's only a reflection of you, you humans, coming back on an alien species, you dumb shit. You feel for nothing. When it comes to humans, <u>I</u> feel for nothing. The main flaw with Metalaw? It's anthropocentric, duh! It's all 'based' on your own dumb selves. So, you give a damn about these kids? I don't. I'm going to *destroy millions*, brats, women your miscellaneous 'innocent man' (all dozen of them). As a for-instance, when your high, through drugs, your happy. Happy, right? That emotion is what you live for, see, that dopamine? You are hedonists, all. Then, when they are gone, when the 'high' is over, then they (the drugs) are evil. Evil! You look back at this dependency on those drugs and you lament, but what are you doing? If you're so hopped-up on methamphetamine, why do we need Adderall? It's the peddler's choice. Why do you think all those pharmacists are <u>satisfied</u> with their stupid jobs? They *sample*, dumbass! This is thesis, antithesis and synthesis coming together in your very brain, Brian. You're so simple, so very simian, you don't understand. I'll show you suffering you can't believe, so watch and learn. And why am I so cruel? What can motivate a creature with my galaxy-collapsing-and-expanding mind to do *such*? To be so punishing, harsh, hard-core, brutal, callus, unkind, unnatural, mean and nasty? Because I <u>fucking</u> feel like it! I'll eat, sexually or otherwise, the whole lot of you humans, and just <u>forget</u> the taste of you. All humans have too much preservatives to be any good. 'Do as thou wilt,' right? I'm an anarchist, and I'll decide *what* <u>cruelty</u> really is. And you mere monkeys? I'll eat your brains (my little Brian) at any Manchu Han Imperial Banquet, which I'll set up. I'd kill God, I'd kill the Devil, good that they don't <u>show up</u>, because they are just sad-fucking-fiction. You creatures are ants beneath my powerful, iron heel. Your religious shit has nothing for me. All is 'known'? Don't be fooled. Mankind is a buffet set-out for the Master of Dread. *Hellraiser* and that Aleister Crowley fool? I'll show you ultra-Hell and Crowley's just my idiot road-<u>die</u>!

At this complete lunacy, I thought Danillia needed to be committed, and that immediately.

What asylum could hold her?

There are <u>none</u> that can.

Could her 'devotion' to anarchism be a defense? Now I was convinced that dragons couldn't be on this Earth. The crazy creature underneath me was only *one* of the reasons why. Would Crocodilians be any better? We didn't need nuclear war, some accident or dictator or sociopath somewhere? If a single Crocodilian could do this, my God, what had I done, trying to save human-kind? Shit the reverse was done. All benighted me, then: I'd created a collection of future-monsters.

As the dragon star reached China, off the shores of Taiwan, right across from it, 130 or 140 miles away my full-dread cindered me (to a dragon-crisp). Didn't China think of Taiwan as a 'rogue' province? China hates things 'out of order'? You'd think Danillia wanted her arrival to be no big deal. Not so. She wanted everyone to bow, that's right <u>bow</u>, to her superior saurian entrance.

And <u>bow</u> all Chinese did, and that instinctively, automatically. Immediately I wished I'd had Sheeta here, or Jing Chang and some of their friends, but no! They'd gone off with their companions, leaving Earth. They didn't want to see their saurian-companions corrupted by mankind's corrupted ways. They knew what humans could be. If they'd known what a crazy dragon actually was, I'll sure they'd have been helping me.

Danillia arrived in China with a meaningful flourish. She was about business, something I couldn't foresee, but I did expect the worst. The bowing Chinese had Danillia in the Great Chinese Hall and were at sixes-and-sevens about <u>what</u> to do with the great beast. A dragon star visiting China, and without their companion, Jing Chang? Thing was, that wasn't the companion to Jing, but I couldn't address it, for the obvious reasons.

They had a hard time just communicating with Danillia. The saurian had no patience at all, insisting that everyone supplicate before her, just like any and all Queens. Hastily, they sent up a Royal Throne Room for her, at a hellish speed. They had no cares about the human manpower needed. A dragon star commanded them.

–Ah! What ceremony else? What are your servile wishes today? Come on, come on get going. Make your foolish entreaties!

At length, not mastering Universalian, but trying to, they communicated their distress over the "aircraft carriers" off their coast. Danillia, resting on the thronal base, only an hour-old, suddenly stood to her nine-foot height, seizing <u>two</u> officials off their feet by their lapels.

She shook them rigorously, all the Chinese leaders looked on, rigging their hands ridiculously. I just stood in one corner, totally embarrassed, thinking hard, and getting nowhere. Danillia's 'environment' still surrounded me, I could do nothing but…observe. I'd never felt so inept as a companion before. Thing was, I was not the companion to Danillia. That role belonged to Jason Shireman. Strategically, maybe purposefully, he was not around.

–Speak, fools, what are you trying to say, before I spill your insides all over this nice red rug?

They indicated that Taiwan and Japan were 'enemies.' All that Danillia needed to hear.

She threw the officials out of the window with a crash. Danillia had no more concern for them, just like a sociopath should. Then she turned on me with a whirl.

–We've work to do; come on, sit on me and enjoy the festival and no flatulence, or I'll fist your sphincter!

She turned, of a huge sudden. In that whirl, Danillia strategically splattered me all over the floor with her mighty arm. A 60+ inch Herculean might, five foot across and around, met my head, flattening me. It felt like running into raised iron, draconian steel, completely at Danillia's (controversial) mercies. She didn't even let her 'environment' defend me.

–Goodness me! Diddum's fall down? Are my fantastic biceps too beaucoup for you? Come here, you scandalous teenager.

She nonchalantly raised me up, just a sterling fork sticking nuisance-meat, pasting me on her muscular back. A grabbing saurian hand, as big as my whole chest, cleaved around me, not caring about the fang-like nails digging in.

I had no idea what to do, sadly 'pasted' on the sinews of a lunatic saurian. The entrance roof of the Great China Hall just blew off. Danillia rose and then rose again: A giant, winged dragon star, growing well-past Godzilla.

–It's time for my greatest performance yet, attend! Our aircraft carriers await. And now, last act, my final stallion-powered-fire! As for grabbing you, and my claws <u>clawing</u> you, my Rights begin where your Rights end. And I've Rights over everything, the Alpha and the Omega, hence your presence on my divine back. You know what they say about Taiwan and Japan, right Brian? I'm going to *trash-shit*! You think that Genotdelian was the Devil, well, Devil this! To hell with all this anime, right my captured human? You won't believe it, prepare to lose your lunch again. If you splatter on me, however, I'll eviscerate you. Betelgeuse, beware!

The star dragon took to the sky, and at 6,000 feet, she acted. Danillia launched, rocketed a fire as hot as any mega-sun, right at Japan, with orange, yellow and a subtle green, inundating all the islands with a flicker of flame rising, then mashing down into

Taiwan. That was over 1,300 miles away, but the draconian mega-burst landed true, submerging and engulfing that whole nation in a *Tsar Bomba* field of unimaginable flame.

–No big deal, the Japanese Islands are up in a fireball that will scorch the outer atmosphere and then, why, we'll get started! Look at Taiwan, 'the darkness of the death bird was blown away,' right Bri? Wouldn't that just make Sheeta Miyazaki and Nausicaa Lee's day? Shame we can't bring them into our story for tearful lament! Look at all these Asians, horrifically dead as winter mud. Just think, all this with one Lizardanian spell, to keep those loser dragons in their self-satisfied-darkness, while the whole Earth suffers my wrath. If the saurians knew of my power over them all, with the exception of Soreidian, this is the *Power of Ruse*, I'd be Outcast from the Earth. But then, where would all the <u>fun</u> be?

Danillia strained herself, poising for the Eastern World to see, doing a *Hulk-stier*, I knew that this was one of the most muscle-overloaded-females that ever was. The saurian stationed herself on the top-most building in Beijing, looking at the raging fire consuming Japan, and, with her eagle eyes, the same-self decimating Taiwan. This was my thousandth time I regretted climbing on her enstrengthened back. Danillia's massive arms were the size of a football field. Her whole body, Olympian times 100(0).

–...and add an additional '0' on the end of the last sentence, too. I also got all the 120,000 visitors to Japan, an added bonus on our humanitarian tragedy (if your me). I can't believe I didn't start this in Book One, what was I doing? I really <u>did</u> mean to do it. Littorian, Korillia, Clareina, Larascena, and the other dumb ass lizards and worms aren't here to defend you. Oh, of the people I just wiped out of existence, didn't you feel their souls 'passing' (by)? Sort of like passing gas, and if I feel some caressing my muscled, Pegasus-strong-back, I'll paddle your ass with nine-inch nails. I'll rip you to tatters in any evening breeze. Sometimes a cigar is just a cigar—say that to 'yon phallus,' right? Some think your loins 'deliver' your soul into others? For me, well, that *could* be right. Too bad that humanity is on my dinner plate, and I've just had a great serving. Well, that takes care of Taiwan and Japan. Two ships sunk by my ultra-saurian-fire-power. I'm satisfied with my 125 million Japanese killed and 24 million Taiwanese obliterated. Forward to snuffing you, Brian Miller Human, it's about past-time, don't you think? As you see, the human public was not shocked, literally no one did anything. No one has even noticed the extinguishment of all these humans? The Japanese islands, all of them, completely destroyed and a saurian spell covering it all up. Isn't it fantastic? Isn't a Lizardanian's magic majestic? I mean, we don't know magic instinctively, as thoroughly as an Alligatorian does, but some of us are trying. The 'newness' of it all: All humanity was possessed by this spell. Can I contain it all within my web-of-magic? Look at all that luggage and cell phone shitbaggyness? Should be thrilling to see how long my spell will last...but NOT for you, attend!

The dragon rose, returning the way we'd come, the Pacific Ocean passing by. Then something occurred to me. I was Danillia's prisoner, no doubt there. Thing is, she was a female. Maybe, just maybe, the same kind of intimacy I had with Larascena and Clareina could be utilized on Danillia. I leaned over to her, again countenancing her right saurian eye.

–My esteemed lady, you know me well?

–Well enough just before I destroy you utterly.

–Very good, my queen. You know about my shortening everything down, due to my simian nature?

–I know about that. We have to be tolerant of our pets. Since you'll be destroyed soon, it doesn't matter. At least, not to me.

–Great then, my eminence. Then let's further impose. May I call you "Danny," for short, my notorious and mega-brutal queen?

She blinked, my 'shortening' being solicited just on her. The complement she shrugged off. Thinking of obliterating the ameba on her enstrengthened back, Danillia giggled.

–Danny? You want to call me Danny now? Hu(man) you really need to be killed, thank the gods, it will be by me. Didn't you know my name was already shortened in Universalian to appease your teenage predilections? Just for that, I'd like to squeeze my hands into your little mouth and open your jaws to dislocation and maybe beyond that? Easy, peasee! Oh, such, such were the joys! That way you'd bleed out so slowly? As an added bonus, I'll just consume your blood, to get the energy out of you, Clare, Lara and Littorian, my little willing reverse-vampires, right? What do you call Littorian, for short? 'Litt,' perhaps? As in 'Little'? I've an added-additional beef with you, he should not be Lord of the Lizardanians. Oh, alright, for now. You've my permission, I'll be your "Danny," and your demise. Another spell possessed Danillia then, the *Monologue Ghost* seized the ultra-Velociraptor. Once again, as Japan and Taiwan burned to a mere cinder below us, Danny turned herself around. I felt the tell-tale scales sliding by, and the massive hands moving up to my hips.

—And we will finish with *yon hipsters* if you—

—But my lady! What of the Dyatlov Pass Incident?

—The what? What's that? Speak up!

—I've not told you of that, my esteemed queen? How rude of me not to mention that, please let me explain. Could you squish me hereafter, oh, that's better my lady. Can you turn back around? Oh, that's going too far, well in 1959, a group of nine, fit, dexterous young people went into the Ural mountains of Russia and horror was to follow. I give to you, my mighty (and please, merciful) saurian queen, the Dyatlov Pass incident. And how can I tell you of this story? Well, it's through the camera pictures and on-site journals. We actually know what happened to these youthful skiers, as you'll hear. At the Ural Polytechnical Institute ten students really wanted "grade three," the most prestigious hiking certificate in all the Soviet Union, and this is their motivation to go. They left any kind of drugs and stuff like that behind, you know, like Vodka and cigarettes, so serious was this sojourn. Their goal: Reach the mountain of Goro Orton, listed at the top of difficulty. On the 25th of January, they started out. So, where are we, my gracious queen?

—Ah, we are almost at the Marshall Islands, but speak on, Hawaii, my destination-next from there, I'll have me a ton of Hawaiian Bowls, too, about a million and a half people, I can see those humans sizzling, too bad you won't be around to see it.

–My Atlantis-mighty-and-superior-saurian, it follows hard upon. Hawaiian Bowls, wow, good plan! Dyatlov mentioned to Yuri that he'd send a message back, a telegram—

Danillia grew anxious.

–What's a telegram, be quick!

Danillia hadn't got her massive hands off my hips, and she shook me, seeking an answer.

–My dearest lady, it's like, uh, a message? Stop shaking this noddle out, please, so I can continue?

Only slightly satisfied, Danillia was urgent.

–Proceed, then, proceed!

The dragon star was growing antsy, not a good sign for me. She had a habit of cracking her massive knuckles, sounding like a thunderstorm, and she did so again. Then, she moved them back to my middle section, tightening slightly.

–Yes, my eminence. Well that tele—that message—never came, because something really went wrong, as you'll detect. Anyhow, Yuri Yudin's backing-out saved his very life. There were then seven men and two women. Igor Dyatlov was in charge of the group. He was respected and well-informed, a good leader. Because it was January and February, the weather was bad, see, my lady? Yudin reported the group as missing so by the end of February, a search party when to Dead Mountain, or Silent Peak, or, as known by the Mansi people, who lived there, as *Kholat Syakhl*. The rescuers located the tent alright. But the tent was cut open from the inside!

At this, I got down level with her huge, and wild and (really) yearning eyes. Probably anticipating killing me, the delight it'd cause. I stared down into the dragon's massive left orb. You wouldn't think a saurian face can be muscular, but it definitely was. Green, blue, and a little yellow, fought in a defined-eyelid-stream trying desperately to show their dominance over everything and everyone.

Years, no eons, of amazing strength rippled and pulsed between and beneath those scales around her amazing, Equestrian head. Many more years than either Lara or Clare, I thought, with a lump in my throat. <u>Years</u> were revered in saurians, the older the (far) better. Still, she fitfully waited, all enraptured with my story.

Danny sighed and said whimsically this.

—When you give your 'opinion,' when you 'opine' on something, you have to respect those who would listen to you, star dragons will listen because you're a companion, your Littorian's companion, see? It's position, not really story. All connections? You bet it's true, even among us reptilians. You're not being a genius, you're being a secret dope, and the longer you keep dragon stars here, the more your people are biting the brink of a shit sandwich. 'Course now, it's too late.

—So please you, Danny, can I go on?

—Yes, yes. Pre-unbeknownst to you, I'll get you back for that Name-Shortening-Shinola, but speak on, why don't you?

—They were scared so badly, they slashed their own tent. All nine of the hikers were found, in the appalling snow, leading away from the tent sight. None were dressed for the negative 30 below-zero temperature. Organized, and single file walking, and that was strange indeed. The bodies were found in the trees, and the trekkers were mangled. Hypothermia was the cause of death, but that isn't the whole story. Bodies were moved, and then the searchers found Igor Dyatlov. He was found face up, both hands made into fists, as though he was fighting someone—or some... *thing*! He was cut up, cut up bad, and missing his jaw incisor. All of the hikers were very messed up, fighting something much stronger than any human. Radiation was a factor in this too. This was all caused by...

At this, I stayed silent.

—By what? Come human don't leave me hanging or I'll definitely hang you!

–The military. The military killed them all, because these hikers were very near…

–Near what, what, come on you gorilla-gerbil-bottom-feeder?

–A wormhole, my lady. The Soviet Military had uncovered a wormhole and they still don't know what it really is. It's in a cave, on Dead Mountain. They secretly want a dragon star, maybe even you, to come out there and explain it all to them. This wormhole might lead into the past. So, where are we now?

–Don't worry about it. And don't go-out so quick, my sub-simian. I've a secret spell to bring you back from the Dead (if applied quick enough). And you definitely don't want this spell—it will make you welcome your end. You know what L.R. Brower said: 'Perfection comes from just existing.' Let's just see if that's true. Death Incarnate might find you, and you can still die by violence. For now, I'll decide when and where you die.

Danillia squeezed my hips together with her unmatchable hands-and-claws (with some delight), then, of a sudden, she noticed me smiling.

–I know it's a bad omen, just when I'm about to overcome all the saurian cherry in you, watching it burst asunder, when skin is cut wide open, but why are you grinning, gorilla-face?

–A moment to answer, your highness? –Ah, that's granted.

Looking briefly around, they were over the Marshall Islands, 3,000 feet up, her wings majestic, gliding on the smooth sky, Danillia <u>did</u> relax her grip just barely.

–I would tell you the tale of <u>The Terror</u> (and the Her Majesty's Ship Erebus), which would mesmerize you again, only you don't have time to hear it.

–I'll be the judge of time here, ass-scratcher.

–At least I've got <u>my</u> evolutionary ladder intact, which is strange. And *Strangely Enough*, that you do not?

A spirited reply did not issue from the reptilian just then. I was whisked away, seemingly by magic. It was Kerok, the wisest Alligatorian and he literally saved my life, him swooping down from on-high. Katrina was my orchestrator. I wonder if she's getting tired of doing that? She got the magic-induced dragons to <u>see</u> what was going on. It took some time. But she did it. Danillia was leapt-on by furious dragon wings, knocking her bodily down into the Marshall Islands by three sets of wanton talons. Larascena, Clareina and Littorian had arrived. The thunder crack alone could have deafened anyone. The supremely surprised Danillia was "descended" to Eneko Island, as Lucifer brought down to Earth.

Only intervention from Soreidian and the cream of the saurians' 20 Lizardanians saved Danillia, then. They had a spaceship standing by and all of them were gone. Larascena, Clareina and Littorian just let them go, and good riddance. I just nonchalantly blew it all off as Danillia being in a mood, brightly smiling to the downcast (but friendly) dragon stars.

They had a lot of work to do.

It took them well over a month, but the saurians <u>did</u> do it. All of this reptilian destruction, they brought back. Japan was a miracle, but they timed it so the annihilation, for those returned from the nether-world, never *really* happened. Same with Taiwan and all the destruction Danillia caused. All the '*tourons*' when back into a normal, bourgeoisie existence. Teresian was suggesting they go back in time, but hesitance was the rule. The punishment was that Danillia couldn't return to Earth—and any saurian could see (or not see) to that end! Not a bad punishment in Danillia's estimation. She hated, really hated me. She should have finished me, but my damn, canonizing, stories! They delayed her.

Oh, the defeat of dragons on their silly, diminutive whims; puzzles and stories, physical pride in themselves, a 'little thing' in gems, action without thinking ahead, and (the notorious) wishing themselves as gods (sometimes forgetting, conveniently, the small 'g').

In fact, no Alligatorians nor Lizardanians would be on Earth much longer. I thought my salvation would be in friendship with the Crocodilians and, maybe, the Wysterians. I had Asians in charge of that, cutting against the grain, one more time. But of my Danny, I shuttered, if she was alive in the Universe...

...she'd get me.

And by violence, too, even in our sleep, it's a 'violent act' if you <u>really think</u> about it. Danny *would* get me.

And any <u>fool</u> can see that.

ONE

THIS CRIMSON BEACH

—*A Taarakian! We have captured a Taarakian!*
—*A Taarakian? Are you sure?*
—*Yes, your Holiness!*
—*But the Taarakian race is dead…extinct.*
—*She has the marks, Holiness. I saw them.*
—*Have her bound…and washed. Then…bring her to me.*
—*And what of the bird?*
—*Kill it.*
—<u>*Heavy Metal*</u>, *Taarna captured (1981)*

In a world with no sound, their cries go unheard. The reality of life becomes totally absurd. The counting of time is considered a crime. And the money one earns, not worth a lone dime. So here they will lie for the rest of the night. Their bodies remain still in darkness and in light. But don't be afraid for it will happen to you. When all will stop as your body turns blue.

—As quoted by Dr. Francis B. Gross (Michael Carr), <u>Faces of Death</u>, a poem by Luther Easton.

As told by Brian Miller's Black World Sword:

...and it's <u>not</u> that I'm good at telling stories, particularly. Yet, I'll give it my best. Sometimes you need the female touch.

See, I can tell, just by reading a few pages, when a *male* has written your tale, or a *female* is the author. Females are more pleasant, more 'flowery' in their descriptions, have greater imagery. Men get right to bad-assery, the grizzly details. If I'm fidgeting into sexism there, well, then I've sinned.

So settle into reading an account told by a female Black World Sword, right? This will be brief, like humans coming (literally) apart, I assure you of that! Good that dragons won't be infesting your world, you be the judge (and jury). Leave the executioner to me.

As soon as the Alligatorians and Lizardanians left on their stupid ruse, that is, going to see the starship *Mixcoatl* on Mercury, and all saurians left this Earth immediately, Brian went back to his office, with me, his *double-edge-femme-fatale*. No one ever thought to ask *me* what I thought about Genotdelian, the Lord of the Crocodilians, and the lie he told to Littorian to get him to see his friend Grendel, the Sereeian captain, in trouble. Even saurians and humans can be dummies, sometimes! The Lord of the Lizardanians was convinced he'd be saving his comrade. I remember what Brian told me, trying to get me not to worry that a major trick had been performed.

–Shoot, 20 or 25 minutes? What could happen in that kinda time? We'll soon have Tiperia overhead, so don't worry. With <u>her</u> here, zilch can happen. She'll appear and give any Crocs a quick dip in the ocean, or something. There's nothing to worry about, my sword, so quit! I can call Littorian back any time *there is* trouble here, so lighten up, silly girl!

–Yeah, but it will take almost half an hour to get those saurians back here. So, should I look around? Maybe report back?

–You, my sword? Oh, come on! Quit trying to swallow a stick

sideways. You hang with me, heck, nothing's going to happen, right, my friend?

–Alright.

Brian was hard at work for about two to three minutes. Most was looking over communication requests by the humans. Someone knocked, politely, at Brian's door.

The distress call was, of course, faked, and so were the images sent to Littorian. An evil expert was the source of images Littorian would misinterpret. The trickster must understand how a young saurian leader would react to such images. It was a simple plan. The author was no less than Genotdelian, Lord of the Crocodilians. I guess I give advice, but, damn, they are dumb sometimes.

A Crocodilian entered and looked curiously around. It was Zaafielian. He perceived me, stepped back, looking at the two of us.

–Now, now. I know how quick you are, my Black Sword. I've come in relative peace, for my part. Mr. Brian Miller, Genotdelian wishes an audience with you. I didn't want to come here, but I didn't like the sparring alterative.

With that, the Crocodilian slipped away.

My human then sunk down, realizing he'd been tricked. Brian quickly communicated to all the human companions in the area. Then he called out to all saurians…and they were minutes away, maybe 20 or 25. But what minutes those were (to become)!

There were 30 companions.

Brian thought to them all.

Lay down your weapons, and I'll negotiate for you. Any other choice, well, these are dragons. You have complete freedom, do as you want, but I've got to fight for you, can't you see that fighting is a noble thing to do?

After all, these were training swords, only, not from my world. None of these humans had a chance to visit my Black World to get the five weapons all wished to have: A sword, two knives, and two hatchets. With that armada, any human would be (almost) invincible. Brian implored the humans to give in.

Really, they had no choice. If they had time to get to the Black World, things would be different. Right now, everything was useless—except maybe me, but I had to protect Brian Miller.

Any weapons just lying about would be as playthings against the Crocodilians. All else went with the friendly saurians. Nothing could penetrate their scales. The human weapons would be toys to a seasoned Crocodilian. After, looking curiously down at the pile of companion swords, a nine-foot-tall Crocodilian reached down and picked one up. The humans drew back a little. It didn't take him much effort to snap it in half, and then snap the two broken pieces again.

Maybe Brian misjudged Zaafielian. He didn't know. These were unfriendly saurians, and all the humans were in their, sizeable, hands. Brian had me, but even I couldn't protect everyone.

Just use his name! Use Genotdelian's name! You must survive this day—is that okay?

One after the other acquiesced. Brian counted thirty names. Genotdelian observed Brian's thought. And he approved.

Brian left the room and appeared outside. Genotdelian came right up to him. He looked positively impregnable. His thick, 50-inch arms were folded and were Cyclopean writ large. At ten feet tall, and of ultra-thick proportions, he felt fantastic that his plan came off so well. He walked proudly down to the beach, even haughtily. The wind blew in strongly from the shoreline.

–Very good, Brian Miller, and it's nice meeting you again. Oh, what a short time we have, you and me. Let's just try to enjoy it?

Crocodilia, continue the destruction. In about five minutes? Get the companions to the beach, please—Brian Miller will be there soon to collect them. I don't want anything to injury them, make sure you follow my deal on Metalaw, right? That's done.

I heard Genotdelian's mental thoughts, too.

—I give the Lizardanians and the Alligatorians about 12 minutes before they're on to us. You've thought to them too, right, Brian Miller? That's just like you. All starships, to the beach, after the destruction, please. And have fun destroying it! Now, Brian, wasn't our distress signal effective? I like probing Littorian's mind, too. That was fun. All the Alligatorians and the Lizardanians fell for it, which is <u>just like them</u>.

Brian was bitter and ground his teeth.

He urged his sword and other weapons to 'hang back,' something we didn't like. Brian brought the King James version of the Bible along, the gift of Genotdelian. The Lord of the Crocodilians and Brian met, and walked together, down to the beach. We had to hide in the trees, most degrading indeed.

—And there! You see? All the companions will be with you on the beach in a few short minutes. You see, two or three miles away? I see them arriving—and, by my estimation, in good shape, too! I mean, destroying your base is what we initially needed to do. And wow, my Crocodilians are in excellent shape, aren't they? I can see their gorgeous muscles from here, very prodigious. A sight to see, yes, Brian Miller?

Genotdelian, on witnessing his own strapping and noble troops, had a drooling waterfall pouring from his massive mouth. He was scarcely aware of it.

—Do you see them, Brian?

—I'm afraid my eyes can't quite see through the morning mist, my lord.

—Oh, well. You'll see the companions shortly.

—What is it now that you want of me?

—Oh, my! Now, how about something short, eh, I heard you like that, shortening the names of saurians down to something you can pronounce? Repeat after me: What do you want?

—What do you want?

—That's better, isn't it?

—Yes, my lord. That's better.

–And what would Larascena say? "Just so," right?

–Yes, my lord.

Genotdelian smiled.

–Oh, I see. You're being watched, right? I'd rather have a good demolisher at your side.

Brian recalled all the things his sword had to say about a demolisher or a spreadem gun. He recalled his sword's words.

Any weapons you have are like a toy to me. Anything—a nuclear weapon, a spreadem gun, a rocket, an Uzi, a whatever-the-hell you have, I'd pulverize them all!

–Littorian, your companion, is just so stupid. He shouldn't be the Lord of the Lizardanians. It's just, well, he's sort of strong, I guess. And we have a long-running war. He wouldn't be anything up against me, mind. You're Black Swords, these are weapons I can respect! They are mighty, and you are so lucky; you'll find that out soon enough.

–It's whatever you want it to be, my lord.

–That sounds, a little suspicious.

–I'm sorry, my lord.

–Littorian is known, in your language, as <u>above</u> a Nephilim and not an Anunnaki, not a Rephaim, he's the son of God—

–A what?

–Human, you are trying. You have your Bible there? Oh, good. Read Genesis, 6:4.

–But I don't think that—

–Oh, just humor me a moment, right?

Brian opened The Book.

–"There were giants in the Earth in those days; and also after that, when the sons of God came in unto the daughters of men, and they bear children to them, the same became mighty men, which were of old, men of renown."

–Not quite correct, but it'll do for now. And 'giants' isn't a good translation. See now?

–No, I don't.

–The sky gods, star people, didn't you <u>read</u> anything in your low-rent Vermont hideaway? Have you read R. A. Boulay's <u>Flying Serpents and Dragons: The Story of Mankind's Reptilian Past</u>? You've never even heard of the Nephilim?

–I'm sorry. And the *What*-lim? Uh, some of the Bible is, er, controversial. It's, uh, supposed to guide you.

–It's all a mish-mash of Hebrew, Sumerian, idioms and all that kind of gibberish. You don't get it? That's the King James Version. Maybe I should have used the International Standard Version. I know it says "Nephilim" in the Jewish Bible. Littorian is not a fallen angel or whatever. Oh, you can get it all on 'the Internets'—and humans are older than you think; why, isn't everyone?

Genotdelian then laughed, and laughed in a haughty way, at his own, private joke. It made Brian sick.

Brian swallowed the puckish-bird-hard. His mental guard mechanisms were set. For his physical frame, Genotdelian would decide.

–Since your cerebral defenses are up, I can guess your thoughts. I'm going someplace, after our little affair here, right? You know where I'm going? Some place close. Very close. I'm going to Triton, next. Sound familiar? I see you still believe in Littorian and Tiperia, right?

–Yes, my lord. It's my life; I do what I'm told.

–But not 'what you want? I've misjudged you. Mankind, a grotesque accident. You are as stupid as you appear. How marvelously disappointing. I know what to do. You see that? I anticipated it myself—your belief, I mean. I'm really remarkable. I'm such a genius—I'm flabbergasted by even sleeping with my own self, come nut-cracking time. And of women? None have survived a night with me, mind. I wash and wear women all day. It's like Deuteronomy 25:11 and 12? My package bursts them like a saurian balloon; I fill them up to exploding! And you, my human, are a eunuch walking with someone hung like a three-times-horse.

Genotdelian smiled and cynically laughed down at the

human. Brian had ice cubes floating in his veins. Genotdelian's scatological reference irked Brian to no end. In that instant, when their eyes met, Brian saw the loathing, the incredible animosity seething beneath the surface of the saurian. He could crush Brian with a thought. Brian looked away.

—You shake. Have you reason to shake? Perhaps you do. I could just twist your head off? Turn your neck around (and around)? Decapitate you? Crush your brain in? Now, what to do with you?

Three Crocodilians then arrived. They looked at Brian with some curiosity. Their muscles, incredibly dynamic as always, seemed particularly strained at that moment, as though the saurians were racing or performing recently. Brian wondered what got them all excited. It was probably the destruction of the nascent outpost. They smiled deeply with their marble, seven-inch teeth, with a gleam that flashed the sun. Then they looked at Genotdelian expectantly.

—No, leave him to me. Oh, and there are the 30, right?

—Our starships are all in the water, just there. Shall we leave, Lord of the Crocodilians?

—Yes, we'll leave. And have about seven minutes left? Did you complete everything?

—Yes, my lord. You see? There are the 30 companions, waving and smiling, my lord? It's just like you said it should be. Just speaking for me, humbly, I really rather enjoyed my time together with these especial humans, we talked about their future and ours!

Brian looked at the Crocodilian smiling up in his bagel mouth with a blank expression.

—Uh-huh. Well, were my orders followed?

—To the letter.

—Then this is where I leave you, Brian Miller. You're a smart kid. You figure it out. What are friends for? I'll see you again and soon, too!

Genotdelian then playfully grappled and wrestled with his subordinates. They all nudged each other and threw wild, playful punches. The haymakers would have gone straight through a thousand lined-up humans. They walked away, laughing wildly. In seconds, the starships were gone in a blur.

Brian smiled, looking at his Lizardanian boots.

He felt himself, up and down—all there! At least he'd saved them, saved the companions, sure, at the expense of the saurian outpost.

Brian waived to us, at the tree line. We floated rapidly down.

—At least the companions are alright, something to show, if not our base.

Then one, floating hatchet looked at the companions. And he looked hard. Then, he backed up a pace.

Brian saw the first companion on the beach waive and smile to him. The others were standing nearby. He waved back.

—Hey, come on! Last one down there is a rotten hobbit sword and all o' that! Who can beat me over to the companions?

But the weapons *stayed* where they were. His sword turned to the other weapons.

—I will tell him. Brian Miller. Don't go down there.

—Now, say what?!

—Don't go. Lizardanians and Alligatorians will be here momentarily. Let them go. Just wait.

Brian turned back. Still the companion waved and smiled, urging Brian on.

—Oh, chillax. The Crocs are gone! You see them waving? And everything can be rebuilt! You'll see.

—Not everything.

Brian turned again. Brian saw the 30 companions. Then he turned back to the weapons, with a quizzical, half-smile. Then he turned back to the humans.

He took a few steps—turning cold and chill, chiller, chilliest. In the bright sun, he saw something red. The sand was running with ensanguined ruin and engulfed in a terrific monochrome of blood. The sea smeared it around in a wide, elliptical pattern.

—Oh, my God!

Brian ran pell-mell down to the beach, to the 30 humans. We weapons followed. He then stopped, glued to the spot like any bug on fly paper. The sea, blood-veined, was up to his ankles.

Every human was dead—but they were *more* than dead. Or maybe so profoundly *less* than dead. They were standing up, looking with eyes glazed over at Brian, looking at nothing. Their bodies had all their limbs—in the wrong places.

To the waiving, smiling and gesticulating human, no fewer than a dozen birds were attached. They were little birds, too, no bigger than starlings. The birds had fine strings on their feet. The excited flapping away of wings caused the waving hand (or *foot!*) on the lifeless human.

The front assembly of companions faced Brian. The teen's eyes were gone, inserted into their cheeks. Male and female, it didn't matter to the Crocodilians—the bloody profundity was frightening. The companion's mouth had somehow vanished, revealing only teeth, utterly naked. There was blood painted where the mouth should be, hence the smiling face. The dozen birds didn't want to be there. They had seen the manufacture of the grotesques. Their wings flapped, all in vain. It made the human dance wildly above the waist.

At the foremost companion, Brian stood in wonder. Looking closer, at the torso, Brian saw something else. A huge seashell stood, making a benignly shaped waist. He saw 10 fingers, or half-fingers, either cut off, or immersed in the sand. He turned away. Of the birds, their mouths were cruelly sealed. They couldn't cry out. But they wanted to, wanted to in a most bereft way. The saffron-like hue of the corpses caused a rumbling in his stomach. He knew the others were worse, far worse. They were more grotesque than the companion with the shell-waist, with one foot up, waving at nothing, with the attached birds. The other foot was cracked at the knee, the toes in a ball, at the shell-waist.

Brian knew what a saurian could do, a power incomprehensible to humans. With their smiles, shining in Brian's open eyes, it must have been 'fun' for the Crocodilians. The humans were like paper;

wet, bones-and-blood paper. They didn't even have a chance to scream. The waterfalls of smearing, vicious fluid, as the companions had their bodies dismembered, caused Brian to almost upchuck.

We Black World weapons went up to Brian. We cast an eye at the forlornness. The two knives were visibly shocked. In their experience, they had been at the sight of carnage. No Black World weapons had seen anything on this scale. Brian turned away—the sights of his forlorn defenders was a relief to him. After, Brian vomited so that his skin matched his hair. Then he rose and looked at we, his protectors.

–Okay, my friends, this is what I want done, if you please. I know it will be hard, but of that, later. I want them wrapped in blankets, all. I want graves prepared. There are 30 of them. Knives, you identify them. I know you can do it. I want them on that little hill, right there.

–But Brian, if they've been ripped into pieces, well—

The sorrowful human looked up suddenly. His eyes, secretly crying; his heart, a twisted lament.

–I don't give a shit about their present state. Graves; sword I want them laid out 10 by three, got it? Stone markers in the shape of Tiperia. A cross, joined in an arc, and the cross coming to a point. You know what I mean. You knives, explain to the sword what you want on the marker. The sword will engrave them. Of the birds, free them. Hatchet see about unsealing their mouths. We don't have much time. Our saurians are coming soon. I don't want them to see the humans like this, okay? I don't want them to see this. I want to be standing before them in five minutes. Now do it. If. If. If you, please.

Then, when the weapons departed, Brian turned again to the sea, and vomited still more in the watery sand. It lasted a long time. A pool of oily groceries now formed between his hands. The ocean, mercifully (its sole mercy of the day) washed it away. It was amazing, the carnage of the Crocodilians. The humans just came apart in their demolishing talons and claws.

In three minutes, it was done.

In four, Brian was standing there, double-awe struck.

It was amazing the weapons could complete the task so fast. All the companions were dead, dead and buried. It was Brian's fault. He urged the Companions not to fight. Against the Crocodilians, even for the best-trained, they would have stood no chance. They would have all been slaughtered in the time it's taken to tell you so.

A minute later, the first Lizardanians and Alligatorians arrived. Twelve crafts, now 13, 14, cleared the air with the twisting of their landing. Their ships littered the beach, and crews and passengers dispatched. The fires, Armageddon-size when the ships came in, were extinguished. Repair crews when to work. All knew they'd been thoroughly fooled, but fooled for what, they didn't know.

The skill of the Lizardanians and Alligatorians working together was very great. By sunset, all signs of the invasion of the Crocodilians were a faded memory.

Everything was as before.

But not everything.

TWO

KNOW THY DRAGON STAR SELF

...the race is not to the swift, nor the battle to the
strong, neither yet bread to the wise nor yet riches to
men of understanding, nor yet favour to men of skill;
but time and chance happeneth to them all.
—Ecclesiastes 9:11

The race is not to the swift, nor the battle to the strong,
but to those who can see it coming and jump aside.
—The Rum Diary, Hunter S. Thompson

Twitter is a constant learning experience,
and I will try to do better.
—Stephen King, in a statement

–See ya later, Nature Boy!

I waved back and at some point, during my walk with Littorian,
I waded into the Florida ocean, washing myself, and then continued
our sojourn, without any water clinging to me. An Alligatorian robe

was so amazing. See, I'd just had a session with my reptilian wives. The life-milk I rubbed in the waves can be replaced.

Should be replaced.

And that, soon, too.

Departed from the rivers of it sadly, I lamented, seeing the lifespunk washing away. The tangible spirit, physical panache, the total liquid-élan, lured-leaked, really maliciously shot, out of a mighty saurian, I simply loved it. I felt drained, relaxed, it was so beyond any-and-all drugs, *lovemaking-nature-boy-saurian-style-entire*!

On our beach-walk, before I began walking and interacting with my friend, I saw a random soda can, rolling on the beach, all rusted. I cringed.

I couldn't get down to our Joan of Arc business.

My people were ruining this Earth. I knew it. My companion saw the tin can, too, nothing got by this reptilian, not ever. He was amazing.

And really, <u>what</u> *was* he to me?

Father? Mother? My saurian wives-rolled-up-as-ululating-orgasmic-One-'n'-Only? Yeah, I knew what he was: He was my Forever-Ever-Companion.

I was very formal, just then, with everlasting respect.

–My liege and lord, I've got to go over some business but wish we were somewhere else. This has nothing to do with getting Stevie Nicks to do "Larascena" in <u>Brian Miller Supplemental</u> as a voice-over in an animation production of <u>Brian Miller Supplemental</u>, either. It's really got nothing to do with that, although that would be my greatest joy as a writer, to have Ms. Nicks do a voice-over for Larascena.

Littorian just looked over at me. Was he smiling? Or was he thinking I was as crazy as a loon? He <u>seemed</u> to be smiling, so I put it down as that.

Littorian walked over to the wave-washed soda can, picked it up, and then crushed it into the finest powder. His bicentennial muscles, casually applied, actually percolated my loins! Embarrassed to say, and true, too. Immediately I put a saurian-mind-seal over my 'internal' event. I was embarrassed two ways, to myself, and outside to all society.

Meanwhile, my quirky, quaky words didn't faze him at all, and he just grinned in a toothy way. He thought I was getting some *free advertising* in.

—Sorry for monitoring your mind, just loosely. I'll stop now, too confusing. An FEC? Federal Exchange Commission? What, *me*? Give me more praise than (mere) that, I should think. I don't guess you have <u>time</u> for that ad maneuver, really. Isn't Stephanie Lynn getting old? Alright my companion, where do you wish to go?

—My lord, I wish to go to Anse Source d'argent, in the Seychelles, sort of northeast of Madagascar, one of those remote islands, right around there. I've only seen these islands on the Internet, though, my friend.

—Brief description?

—Uh, okay. Some beaches have a 'feeling,' an aura, well this one has an ultra-mighty-*morphia*, and my full attention will be gripped by this place, so I can, conduct this business concerning our time-travel-trip to save Joan of Arc, my lord. The white sand through my feet, a cloudy day with a certain amount of sun just poking through those palms that are—

—Do they have <u>rocks</u> there?

—Rocks?

—Yes. Boulders, ginormous ones, it will relax me on our talk.

—I think so, my lord, uh, yes, granite pillars in the white sand, sure!

With that, I was seized in his six-or-seven-inch dragon-star talons, GPS was coordinated with his unimaginable mega-mind, magic liberally employed, and we arrived in the Anse Source d'argent near Madagascar. I recovered nicely, crawling off his sleek, muscled back, looking up to the grey and white clouds. The clouds cancelled the sun for prolonged times, I figured I wouldn't be burned (being with a dragon, you <u>can</u> be.)[2]

Interestingly (at least to me) Littorian's strengthened back looked 'different' from Clare and Lara's. You'd think muscle (male) = muscle (female) if you're a saurian-borne. But it wasn't that way. It's just like telling a woman writer from a male writer, just follow me in this rabbit-hole-syllogism. I can tell the difference, eight times out of ten between women writers and male writers. Maybe it's the way they use adjectives and adverbs, I don't know. Yes, I can tell. Anyway, all print journalism these days is a fat girl's dopey diary with the disintegration of paper-media in general.

A saurian woman's muscles just seem *gentler*, more naturally flowing. Being a teenager, you have to make a conscious effort <u>not</u> to fondle a saurian woman's muscles. If you did without permission, you'd lose a hand for sure. Male saurian sinews seem more brutal and bullish. A reptilian woman is as strong as a saurian male, too, forget that at your peril. A saurian woman's muscles are quite a terror if they are cross when employing them, any tragedy can result.

–No one around either, this is so excellent! Like they say about the 'Lords of the Saurians,' they can do anything…what about freedom of speech, my Grace?

I bent down to the sand, and its whiteness almost made me invisible. Looking down, my companion regretted that fact. We were in between Grand Anse and Petite Anse. Oh, just look it up, and be in paradise (for now). Fortunately, there were no people here, it was near dusk. With Littorian, I felt so relaxed, like I could be myself. I was on the pleasant side, too, I've been physically 'drained,' in a great way, by my serpentine wives. Too, I was pleasantly relaxed,

---

[2] But not by a Lizardanian. NOT that fire is an impossibility for them. Only Crocodilians can produce fire as hot as any sun (ever!). And NOT if they are in the 'top three,' you know, the strongest reptilians that ever are (or were, or whatever)—no magic escapes them, including fire. Oh, you've learned that stuff already. Or have you? It doesn't matter. One thing is forever-for-sure: There is no <u>higher</u> wish for a teenager than being a companion to a saurian. Just one flight with one of them, and you can't go no better.

sort of like being drunk in the initial parts, so to speak. Me, kindly obliterated, in a very good kinda way. Littorian added to that feeling of bliss, he was so noble, so divine, he didn't make me feel alienated, not estranged. You couldn't help but be pleasant around a <u>real</u> dragon (star).

–You can do, think and say anything you want. I encourage it. I expect it. I've draconianly taken care of all freedom of speech issues right there! By-the-merry-way, I can improve your appearance, you know. Give me a try, okay? Your wives might like my improvements, right? Please let me try? Taking on two reptilians is a lot for a human to handle.

–But not for a <u>teenager</u>-human to handle, my friend! Just remember, first chummed, first served! My appearance we can 'countenance' at the proper time, my lord. I've never been too much on how things <u>look</u>, just how they <u>perform</u>. I'm thinking that Larascena wants to get back to Beterienna, on her home-world. Her magic has been 'building' up to the point where she can resurrect her from the distant past. That is unprecedented and it's agitating her in the extreme. I'm sure she explained everything to Clareina and maybe she is employing that Lizardanian's magic in the same direction? Beterienna means a lot to Larascena, I know. You remember Beterienna, from the Water World? Well, I know you can bleach my hair another color, and all. Maybe even renew me internally, like you cured my stroke. I've always said you are omniscient and omnipotent. Of that, later. Now, the business I have to discuss?

The green-white-blue waves scuttled at my bare feet and the water rapidly dried away on the whitish sand. All was extremely-serene, and I prayed any soda can, plastic or otherwise, wouldn't appear.

Littorian was a little dismissive, but he did smile at my copious complements (if you knew what to look for; for most, he was always smiling).

–Okay, there are some limits to being a god. Only God Almighty knows no limits. And Larascena doesn't believe in God? I think that's too bad, but I'm an anarchist, by the best-human measure, right? Maybe you can help me there: Thesis, Antithesis (that'd be you) and Synthesis, correct? Oh, let me see, wow, there are many boulders here, very good. I can stand your dragon-business now, just as long as I can entertain myself. All dragons have needs.

–Your magic will right any lives you shatter, my lord?

–Oh, yes. I'm not trying out my Clydesdale-saurian testicules, I'll right-everything, on leaving. Just talk very loudly during the crashing 'n' smashing. I'll listen, you'll see. And remember, there is no beach to walk on, <u>except</u> this one! You feel relaxed now, don't you, talking to me? I do wish to make you comfortable. And that picking up any jellyfish and throwing them out to sea and saying, "It mattered to that one!" is out, I've already learned that lesson from you.

–Alright my lord, let's indeed leave those Zeus-like nards alone, Tiperia can take care of those (go)nad-massives and then some. I'll think of another lesson, anon. The sun in the sky, 72 degrees, it *should* be heaven, but having you in it, it's heaven-plus-+! You're so magnificent looking, it's just my pleasure to be in your humble company, my noble liege.

–Yeah, baby, please keep up the compliments, too, as a good companion should!

–Alright my vigorous companion. I'm glad you stuck by me, on getting saurians to come to Earth. I see now how wrong I was. It's good that, after getting Joan of Arc companioned to Anakimian that all of us just go, my Royal Lord.

Littorian considered.

–Uh-huh, and devious-you, you want Crocodilians to take the place of Alligatorians and Lizardanians to prevent nuclear war on your world? It's good to be wrong with a rational reason. 'Royal' lord? You flatter me. You had this rational reason, and it was <u>reasonable</u>! It's good to be with someone smart and underhanded. And I was 'underhanded' to you, right? But I tried to do you right, know that. Always remember, then you can reflect with added emphasis, then you can have a meaningful eucatastrophe. That's our over-all goal, you know. To understand all is to forgive all—you are at a 'synthesis' that I wanted you to come to, definitely come to on your own. I was glad to support you in this process, but really, I didn't do anything (not being your benign antithesis, Soreidian took that role), in keeping with anarchy (or not!). Now, are we done? Well, good again. Watch this casual display of extreme-awesome power and try not to cream all over yourself, leave that for Lara and Clare!

With that, the creature went over to a granite structure twice the size of a double-decker-bus and lifted the whole thing, quite effortlessly. Littorian's strength, his rocketing, mountainous arms, his staggering biceps and Everest peak just had me trembling. Five feet of muscle on both of his arms, damn. His claws dug into the stone as he lifted it over his head-fins. Every gargantuancy my companion possessed was bulged out in a physical-fantasy-land. I immediately thought of those 'bullworker' ads of yesteryear, the muscular males (and females, too) exercising, every sinew pulsing with power. I just gaped at Littorian in absolute awe-'n'-shucks.

Ground caving in around the reptilian, all kinds of creatures were disturbed from the dragon-star-mightiness towering above them. It'd been some time that I saw my companion 'exercising' and it was drama-unforeseen. His biceps were almost as enormous as Soreidian's or the Lord of the Crocodilians, almost 60 inches around like a carved, sculpted mountain, creasing up in an enstrengthened titanium peak. No wonder he was deified by humans, and yet he was not a Nephilim, he was one of God's chosen angels. Well, I thought Littorian was; so, he was!

Littorian's ultra-green-porcelain-body liked that kind of weight quite nicely, but I've already said that he could take the head of Superman and chow-pulverize that cranium in his supreme teeth, and stamp all over the Justice League or the Avengers until they were dust, with just a mere thought. The strength of this dragon-star could crunch anything. I just can't do any justice to his incredible massivity, he plowed over the human 'heroes' like a Tyrannosaurus Rex (with <u>ultimate power</u>, of course).

–Your mouth is watering a bit, but I won't tell. You're maybe undressing me in your mind? Opps, too late, I'm birthday suiting it. Must have creamily-capped-off your semi-stoppable homosexualism you attempt to repress. You're probably flattering me again, in your brain. Doesn't it get sick of that? Oh, very well. The only thing I *can't* crush would be the love in my heart for you, Brian. I'm not trying to establish any parental tyranny, it's too late for that, but do you see the waves out there, crashing on the round plate of this island, right, about three miles away, my companion?

–I do my lord, it's almost on the skyline, very far away.

I wanted to encourage him, even though I'd seen him as a dragon fighting Genotdelian, the former Lord of the Crocodilians. That was an epic, supreme fight, at least what I saw of it. Thing is, I couldn't get enough of seeing him 'enstrengthened' and that over quite nothing, like now. Like a cup with no bottom, his draconian nature I wanted to bring out. Suitable blame falls on my being a teenager and wanting to see his massive power. My dual wives confronted all of my 'muscling' thoughts, my hours of wrestling around with them, and believe me my thoughts were dirty. Not 'dirty-dirty' (I know, at this young age, the difference) they were based in a <u>love</u> (and some lust) that knew no bounds, with my saurians. It wasn't based on some concept of 'domination,' not that, I just wanted to be 'consumed' with the strength of dragons, I guess. No teenage human could ever ask for more, not if you know saurians, <u>true saurians</u> everywhere and anywhere.

Here, I just anticipated seeing Littorian's juggernaut of super-power. Quite obviously, I would die for Lara and Clare. Or Littorian. The others…well. These three saurians were special to me. Like the Divine Trinity, maybe. No human could appreciate the 'having' of my saurian wives, no human could even 'do that kinda stuff,' it was just awesome and so ineffable. They brought a 'filthy' word like 'sex' to a whole extra level, a new, extra-verified and awesome height, leaving 'filthy' far behind. As a teen, I <u>constantly</u> wanted it! And I'm not being a 'lazy shit' when I call it ineffable, either, so there.

Littorian threw the massive-rock-bulk and it landed (after a very high arc, staying in one piece, maybe by magic, I didn't know, didn't really care) making huge destruction when it impacted. It looked for all the world like a hydrogen bomb, the Everest splash, reaching just below the evening clouds.

Littorian looked satisfied, and his large eyes darted down to bagel-mouthed-me.

—Don't worry, don't worry, I'll restore all the life and decimated land occurring on our little walk.

I set my latent, very subdued, sexual-excitement aside, as Littorian looked around for a much larger rock. I'm ashamed to admit that I had an attraction to Littorian but really, I knew it was benign. I wasn't asking to be the "second" after Tiperia, after all, not another lover. That event I'd never survive, I'd literally be turned inside out, his apparatus was that gigantic. I'd seen him making a whole-lotta-love to Tiperia, and that one incident was awesome(ness) and the Lord of the Lizardanians could fill me up to a positive explosion (in a loving way). Littorian caused me to recognize the Freud in me.

The saurian had his eye on a little mountain that was as large as the capital building in Washington, D.C. As my companion lifted, albeit slow, showing off his gargantuan muscles, a chain of thoughts pulverized me. Indelibly and incidentally, this monumental land-mass(ive) must have weighed in the neighborhood of 10 billion pounds. I'd heard that when someone asked how much the capital weighs. I remember it from a tour I took, during the first part of high school, of the nation's capital. All of him, eight or nine feet tall, was sheer muscle. It was poetic, the saurian lifting this much weight. Of course, I saw him do far more than this, defeating Genotdelian, the previous Lord of the Crocodilians. That Crocodilian must have been infinitely stronger.

This one gigantic rock, thrown with force, proceeded to pulverize the front-plate of the island and set the whole ground to quaking, it went off like a Thermonuclear bomb. The resultant splash was incredible. All of it seemed effortless, Littorian's breathing continued as normal. The saurian smiled with huge-gratification at the mini-apocalypse he set up, is gargantuan hands on his hips.

I got down (finally) to business. He was looking for a much, much larger projectile, and my words halted him (just barely).

–Littorian of course you will have to be immunized. All of you saurians that are choosing to go back in time to save Joan of Arc, I've got the Black World weapons ready to give you the appropriate shots.

–Immunized? No, that's taken care of, my companion. Concern yourself with something other.

–Are you sure, my lord?

The Lizardanian just looked down at me, and then got down to my level, taking a knee. Littorian was kindly, and I felt a familiar and a gentle warmth from him, like no other. It wasn't like my reptilian wives, either. I had ineffable love for him, and my companion could see that right off. For my especial-saurians I felt such affection, a teenager's love that knew no bounds. For him, I felt life coursing through my dragon-adapted veins, and that of life itself, my love of life, it just 'pulsed' out of Littorian and through me. He was a god. He was the reason that I existed at all. Without him, I couldn't go on. I don't know if this 'companionship' exists in human life generally, but I *suspect* it does. It's a need to learn, and to tell what you know—I mean, the synthesis of 'what' you know. The saurians could turn your mind around all kinds of things. They wouldn't force you or any-such-thing. The saurians wanted you to learn for yourself, and, importantly, by yourself.

Littorian didn't want me to be so depended on saurians, didn't even want me to think it, but I did. No, the gods can't control you completely. The Lord of the Lizardanians could destroy whole worlds or create them—and he much, much preferred to create. My love, even though I was just a teen, was complete for my companion.

My mind focused on Genotdelian's 'warping me' into some

kind of doubting my companion, earlier on. To understand all is to forgive all, Tiperia and Littorian showed me a greater truth. That was probably a prime reason Genotdelian killed me. My companion ripped me out of the Grim Reaper's grasp, and that made him more than an angel to me. I'm just a teenager, I'll 'grow up' and get out of such feelings about my companion, I'm sure. But not really, with star dragon blood in my veins, already I could take on 20 or maybe 30 men, my strength growing. My life as a dragon, what would it be like? A different life? Give up on humanity as a dragon? Or can I reach out to them, as a dragon? Can I love being human even if I'm not?

Littorian put his hands on me, dwarfing my arms. He squeezed, but it was a loving squeeze.

–Course! You worry too much, my teenage human. I've thought of everything, as I usually do. I'm a dragon-star after all, have some genuflected deference! I'm the <u>mightiest</u> dragon-star ever, and I <u>might</u> spar with Kukulkan before we are done. We know that much about shape-shifting, everyone will be immune to everything. Of course, I'm not insulted. You care for us, I know. I wouldn't have the power needed to lift any rocks bigger than a Beetle Volkswagen, but who knows, right? I can now, and maybe that's all that matters, the future doesn't really exist? Any acting-up by any given Frenchies, I'll just clod them to near-death. I'm eons older than you, but still considered a 'young' leader of the Lizardanians. Now that the <u>saurian war</u> is over, I can let go of this position as Lord of the Lizardanians (but not the *power*, I'd elect to keep that, ahem!). And that's only in war-time and you, Brian Miller, have single-handedly moved the great saurian community beyond war into the snuggling arms of peace! You are far greater than you know. We adults tend to embarrass the children, or the teenagers. So there, my companion, be satisfied! I'll be a strong, as sinuous as any given bulking-Clydesdale, don't worry yourself about me.

–A Clydesdale is a draft horse and can move 8,000 pounds, my lord. I read that on the Internet(s).

–Just that, 8,000 pounds, my companion? How much can they 'pick up,' I wonder? Well, to get Joan of Arc lifted from that lil' French stake, we must all be prepared to sacrifice. I have my girlfriend Tiperia handling it. Oh, the pains of being Lord of the Lizardanians! Can I stand the strain a moment longer? Your familiar with Star Trek, right?

–Gosh, which one, which franchise, that's like saying Star Wars, I just hope I get my acknowledgements right, writers hate to be plagiarized, my lord?

–Plagiarized, here? We are on our own frontier dealing with dragon-stars, damn. And those 'Gorn' references? Please. Two letters *lacking* there, and you have 'dragon,' totally yuck, and dah. They look nasty and they are slow and don't let me go on about them, I've something *else* to do today. I'm into specifics! Have you seen _The City on the Edge of Forever_?

–Written by Harlan Ellison? I like to give credit where credit is due, my gracious lord.

–Good, good. If we change one thing in time, if one person dies, who knows what changes that will make throughout time. Time has to resume the shape that it has, or maybe even all saurians might never come to Earth. Whether that is for good or ill, you decide.

–I get you Lord Littorian. We'll be careful.

–Both of us will have to be careful, my friend, and we don't like going back or forward in time you understand?

–That wasn't the only time they dealt with Time, my lord. In _ The Naked Time_, written by John D. F. Black, when the ship went into a time-warp, going backwards in time and—

Littorian waved his hand and laughed at himself, myriad teeth raging in the sunlight. Then, he talked of the Supreme God of Everything, the spy systems of the world, the British people, the books I'd read, my articles, my 'quiet revolution,' my utmost thoughts (and his) about everything and every-when, living forever as a dragon, the fact that my Dad walked out on my Mom before (and, ergo, why I was a good companion that-a-way), my family and their 'disposition' (which was cool, he'd take care of them, *par excellence*), and he talked about strings, sealing-wax, and other fancy stuff!

We had a roaring fire that night, (and maybe another night, I can't remember; talking to him was so fascinating, I could do it forever) talking and talking and thinking and thinking! We discussed things through telepathy and verbally.

Littorian 'righted' things at the end of our little couple-of-days-walk. All life was restored, all was fine. After, I was all set on finding Joan of Arc and that everything would go right given that I was amongst gods. How appreciably wrong I was about everything going right!

THREE

GODZILLA? JUST MY ERRAND-BOY!

All that we see or seem is but a dream within a dream.
—Edgar Allan Poe

Larascena, Warlord of All Alligatoria, stared at the huge buildings. The ultra-Velociraptor smiled. Meaninglessly, I spoke (as is my wont).

–Where are the Black World weapons? I'm missing them.

–I don't know.

–Where are the young saurians? You know, geez, the elder pilots? Larascena deftly shook it off. These foolish human questions!

–I don't know.

–Boy, you don't know much.

–Shut the hell up! However, stay close by me, Brian. I'm checking the radiation levels of the city.

–Is it good to go?

Moments elapsed.

–Yeah, it's good enough.

–So, why stay close by you?

–We've already talked about that. You've got no weapons, dummy. I could have my way with you.

–Hey, Larascena.

–Yeah, what?

–Thank you.

–For what?

–You said to thank you when we reached the planet. So, thank you.

–You care about what I say, yes?

–Of course I do.

–Well then shut up, silly teenager-human!

–You'll take care of me, right, my star dragon?

The outrage that hit Larascena was mega-epic.

–I'll staple your mouth <u>shut</u> or just rip it the hell off!

–Then I'd scream.

–I don't have time for your little, and annoying, tangential issues. Sit by your stupid dish!

Brian didn't mention love.

But he did love her, as if love hadn't been invented by anyone else. He felt it back from the saurian, even though she resented it utterly. Larascena wanted to say she was sorry for his mental injury, but her pride prevented it. To Larascena, Brian was just so ridiculous. Still, the Alligatorian couldn't help the way she felt. They'd been through so much. To think, they started off as enemies. Brian Miller was too in love to be <u>this</u> saurians' nemesis.

There was no need to talk about it. The love doesn't need to be mentioned; it just was, and never-ever was not.

That love, a 'temporary love,' was invincible and clung between them like a rigid, steel cord. Whether permanent or temporary, it was unknowable. Larascena could crush it, but did the Alligatorian want to? An indestructible link—but fragile, always given to the feelings they shared. They were volatile feelings. This was unprecedented. Never had a human been in love with a saurian. Larascena was uncomfortable with that, but she couldn't help it. Not with all the strength she possessed. Larascena fought the emotions within her. She found herself fighting a bladed war with—only herself?

Brian smiled at Larascena's frowning face.

–Geez. Okay. You know, it's nice to be cared about.

Larascena was walking to the city, but it seemed like a run to Brian. Her long, extremely handsome legs, stupendous, and high black boots kept Brian at a trot. The star dragon was gearing up, looking at the city. Larascena's large eyes and chiseled face seemed beautiful to Brian. He'd seen too much of her—or maybe not enough.

All around, grey.

Brian saw smoke rising lazily up in one part of the city, now another, very far away. He pulled out his Alligatorian binoculars. They revealed nothing. He took the strap out, letting them rest against his chest.

The two arrived at the city's wharf. A pier stretched out into the dreary ocean. The capital city ran between the ocean on a peninsula. Behind, the steel, black, and moonscaped city looked down on them. Still, some skyscrapers still oppressively stood. Their boots kicked up dust. Long finished, this war. Nothing left but storefronts, electrical lines, hollow buildings and old military vehicles.

–The military stuff is all broken, I see. Created by geniuses to be ruined by me, but I'm too late! I'm going to get out some bumptious aggressions. I'll spare your face. I'd pulverize it anyway, one stroke.

–Stroke? Hey, I've already suffered one of those. Really, it wasn't nothin'.

Brian smirked at the pun. Larascena grumbled.

–I'll slaughter that city. The next eighty blocks look pretty suspect, now, don't you think? I'm going to black hole this wretched town under these inevitable (and enviable) claws.

Larascena tensed up her gargantuan biceps. She was even mightier than on the Water World. Her huge trapezius, deltoids, even down to her strained, muscle-ridged gluteus and hamstrings, all maxed out. Brian had his mouth open again.

–Now, you can gawk at my extremist-fantastic, yes?

Casually, she looked over at Brian, her massive ego on heart-scalding-ultra-overdrive. For the human, remembering the great heights of her arms, it seemed like he'd been looking at someone else. The twin peak-points were incredible, past the bulbous position of merely patting them or stroking them. Larascena had to look up to see that scale-ripped crest crescendo on her arms. The veins were actually pulsing beneath marble muscle—pushing the scales up.

Larascena stretched her impregnable self—now ready for action. Her sinuous tail was pining for the adventure of smashing, crashing and whacking the hapless metropolis.

–I'm *starving* to get at this benighted Kalashnikov culture. Do you know how many muscles I have in this tail?

–Uh. About 38.

–About 48! Now, count them.

–Well…

–I'm waiting! You're slowing up a Warlord wanting to get busy. Just <u>look</u> at that city—an Alligatorian Warlord will finish it, and then off the map. I'm waiting now!

Brian counted as she held up her tail for him. The muscles where ripped with little cords of veins, pulsing out the scales. He couldn't believe that he didn't notice her tail before. This was probably the prime of her power, the most intoxicating of all immortal toxins, this appendage.

–Well?

–Yup. 47.

–<u>What</u>??!!

–I mean 48.

–Now, just so!

She consoled herself with the coming Sedan of destruction. After all, no one would be killed, of course. Well, duh!

–Care to try a finger in these Samson abdominals? Let's try an arm. I'd break it and clean off. Any coins you might have about your person, I'd not only fold them, I'd break them.

–Frickin' wow.

–Impressed? Am I not a huge, giant-size Atlantean Percheron?

–A what?

–It's sorta like a horse, geez.

–Oh, yes; a beautiful, singularly muscular horse, too! It's like I didn't even see you before. You have the most awesome body I've ever seen on any saurian, anytime!

Larascena cooed. She luxuriated in the human's mystical connections, Brian's favoritism and extreme partiality, just the things he said. She was more fascinated with Brian than he knew.

–Just, just so.

–Hey!

–Now what?

–I can drive that.

–Drive what?

–Drive that jeep. No not that one; that one is finished. Yes, there, that one.

–Are you sure?

–You just watch.

Brian walked over to the jeep. He removed the dead bodies. You couldn't even see what they were—humanoid or alien. He didn't investigate. Brian put them (gently) on the ground. There wasn't much left.

It wasn't that dissimilar to a normal jeep. It was a stick-shift. He pushed the clutch in. Brian started it up. It responded like new. Was it gas-driven? He couldn't tell. He hopped out. Brian circled the jeep. He saw some exhaust—but it didn't smell like gas. It smelled like—well, nothing!

Meanwhile, Larascena was getting impatient. She removed her boots, strapping them on her belt, as Brian sat in the jeep, figuring things out.

Larascena scratched the ground with her mighty talons.

Twelve inches of earth moved. She drove it out of her way. Yes, her reptilian-self was about to have a work-out, as she smiled up to yesterday's-buildings.

–You got it working! Good. So much exhaust-smut for this world's miserable atmosphere?

–Look at this action.

He popped the jeep into reverse. Brian backed up over to her. Just then, Brian had a movie in mind (as was <u>his</u> wont).

–Now, y'all sure you don't want a ride?

Larascena put her hands on the jeep. Sinking and squishing it down to the ground, slightly.

–No thanks.

Larascena then lifted the whole jeep, over her head. She noticed the underside of the jeep, gave a little laugh, and then nonchalantly set it down.

–Heavy, ain't it?

Larascena's scaly eyebrows rose.

–What? Are you kidding me? I could throw that thing to the several moons, like to see?

–Look, Lara, here's the deal. Let's play a game. I drive ahead and you try to catch me, see? It's like a puzzle; you never know which way I'm going to go. But I promise to go north, see? That'll give you a chance to knock down those buildings, right? If I see any standing up, you lose, right?

–Well, that should be refreshing enough. You don't even have a sword to defend yourself, if you make me mad.

–Oh, make you mad? So that's it. Hey, you know something?

The engine revved up. He found first, second, third, fourth, with the clutch down. He had it in second, to start. Brian smiled.

–You know something? You're looking a little slow Lara! What's that? Is that—what—fat I see? A layer (or two) of celluloid I see on that midriff?

Larascena smiled slightly. She looked down at her stomach. Ten extreme ripples of solid, extreme muscle, fat only lived (vicariously) in the dictionary; but she wanted, *needed*, to be goaded, nay, *egged*, on.

–Wow. Well, well. Fat, eh? What happens when I catch you?

Larascena looked on, pathetically.

–Then…well…you can *Eat Me*!

Brian took off.

The jeep spat back a ton of dirt and rot all over Larascena, head to tail. The military vehicle roared off.

For some reason, she laughed.

Her great head and fins rocked back, and she laughed hysterically. Then, she pounded the ground with her tail, continuing to laugh.

WHHAAAMMMM!

It shook the outskirts of the city. It was probably a 9.5 or a 10.0 on the Richter scale, all buildings shaking, some crumbling.

Brian, mistakenly, thought Larascena was coming on fast. He pressed the gas down hard, and the jeep responded. Driving almost hysterically, he avoided all kinds of cars, military vehicles, roadblocks, twisted things, all kinds of muck-and-truck. And alien dead figures. Those were the worst. On Brian's wild ride, there were lots of them. If he'd known about these dilapidated bodies, he wouldn't have suggested the game. They were black, indistinct, but he knew what they were.

Brian needed to get Larascena's aggressions out. He knew about the predilection of games and riddles in the saurian mind. Chasing a jeep down (then eating, in a good way, the driver) would be just the thing to exhaust the Warlord.

When Brian looked into the review mirror, he couldn't believe it.

Larascena was imitating Godzilla, only with a myriad of massive muscles. And moving, much, much faster—Brian had a Warlord Alligatorian on his tail. Larascena was a monstrous size, as big as any building. He'd seen her grow like a Titan once before. This giant Larascena was what the machines faced on the Water World. No wonder they were all destroyed—well, she got them down to two.

Brian's hunger took a second seat to visiting the bathroom.

Number One, Number Two and vomiting were scheduled for the gross-out room. But not now; to run away, that was his best defense.

The destruction Larascena created! Buildings were pulverized, utterly. She joined both mighty, leviathan hands together and bounced buildings into each other, creating a domino effect. All the buildings on either side of her were obliterated and then some. There was a sea, on both sides of the city. Literally, the buildings piled up in the vast waters. Huge smashes of ocean from the destroyed structures, reflected in Brian's shaky review mirror. But it slowed her down. Her tail took care of the rest, creating an earthquake, shattering everything down to the ground. Larascena shouted through her laughing:

–YOU WANT TO BE EATEN, BRIAN MILLER?! WELL! AND NEITHER WILL A SILLY OLD VIRUS DESTROY YOU, LAMBDA, BA.2, EBOLA, OMICRON, DELTA, ALPHA VARIANT, SARS-COVID-WHATEVER, THE HELL WITH THAT, I'LL SWALLOW ALL OF YOU, THE WHOLE-VEINY-THINGY-THING-OF-YOU!

How can something sound so terrifying and horrifying be so hot and exciting?

Brian wondered that, increased speed, the game just <u>had</u> to continue.

Larascena saw Brian's jeep going down the main road, occasionally running into all manner of things. She chuckled and giggled excitedly. Oh, such a game! She must be careful not to hurt him. At the same time, she wouldn't want to lose the wager.

Larascena started hitting the buildings harder and harder—they rocketed back, smashing each other to the ocean. Talk about getting out your aggressions! The war of the past was nothing compared to this treatment. All behind Larascena, everything totally crumpled and wrecked.

Brian was going 65 or 70 miles an hour. Larascena, in giant-form, was close behind. Her steps crumpled everything, and all manner of things were ripped to shreds. Cars and military vehicles sliced up with her mighty claws and powerful talons. Nothing could stop her outrageous onslaught.

He rounded at the corner and needed to get on the straight-away fast.

Then he saw them.

Creatures, by a collection of trash cans, in the middle of the road, a fire lit. You still couldn't tell what they were, human or alien. But they lived here. It was their city—what was left of it.

–SON OF A BIT—

Brian wheeled the jeep around in a donut. It spun through the air. Not strapped in, he would be crushed between the seat and road. His final speed, 72 miles an hour and pavement the end result. Coming up, Larascena stopped her smashing, looking on. She recognized the other life, now scattering into the streets, disappearing before her eyes. As for Brian, there was nothing she could do. Maybe pick up the pieces, see about constructing a whole human again. She froze solid.

Brian was going to hit the street—and hard.

The jeep completed the summersault. Brian stiffened his body. As he flew through the air, he shut his eyes. He saw Death Incarnate, laughing, and reaching out to him.

This is the only world you seem to know. I, Death Incarnate, await you here and now!

Of a strict-sudden, Brian's sword arrived, at hyper-speed!

It blocked the blow of the road, in a complex maneuver. It actually absorbed Brian's fall. The Black sword hulled Brian out of the jeep, lightning-quick. The jeep fell over—with no one inside. It slid into the neighboring building's window bank, shattering panes of glass on the first and second floor. The jeep's gas tank sheared off and exploded like a match. The flame engulfed the lower building, blowing out every window, up five stories. The creatures scattered like any vermin, and ran, literally, into the streets, vanishing.

A block later, Brian's Black World sword set him down. He was accustomed to riding her like any broom.

–You're alright, my human? Well, good.

In answer, Brian hugged the Black World sword and didn't care if he was cut. She wouldn't allow that, instantly shaving her edge back, putting the flat part against him. Brian kissed his sword, passionately, numerous times. She embraced him back, tightly. The sword wrapped her pommel, hilt and guard around him.

–Sword, I'm more than happy to see you! You saved my life.

The sword looked over to the side of the building like a parent staring down a local dragon.

–Well, someone, some lil' saurian, might have been able to assemble you, after you crashed. I rather doubt it. Something would be left out, then where would we be?

Brian hugged her close again—really, really hugged her and wouldn't stop.

–Now, now—it's okay! Calm down, silly human. I have you, right? Nothing's going to hurt you when I'm around. You know, I'd never leave you…not with *her* watching over you. What an absurd, juvenile and hyper-stupid game, I've interrupted, here, Larascena!

The Warlord, at her usual size, was standing at the corner, arms crossed, one shoulder propped up, with her jaw dropped. At the insult, she snapped the jaw tightly shut. She was growling. The fact that Brian suggested the game didn't seem relevant.

–I never thought I'd say this about you, errant sword. I'm, well. I'm glad to see you. Enough said.

In a huff, she turned away. She went back up the street, to look at something. After 50 or 55 blocks of destruction, she was satisfied. Not tired—but satisfied.

Just then, around the same corner, his hatchet and knives arrived, elated. His hatchet screamed out.

–Brian Miller! You see? I knew the sword would find him! I knew it!

Brian celebrated with his weapons. He hugged them all. One

hatchet, two knives—Brian kissed them, holding them, and putting them in his belt. With his weapons, he felt at home. Brian lifted his sword. This Black World sword, one that Can Not Be Named, was the most important sword, anywhere and anywhen. She didn't have a 'name,'—she was simply *She*. He knew how to touch it. One hand, enough—the thumb, ring finger and pinky wrapped around the hilt. Brian's index and middle finger elongated, went up the hilt, settling below the guard. He could feel the tang, fuller, edge with his finger slightly on the guard. With this grip, he felt her strong, confident mind.

–I'm not worthy of you. I'm not.

–I know a certain Lizardanian that will say you are.

–I'd give my life for you.

–I'd give my life for you!

It felt so light in his hand—but it was heavier than it looked. She had a way of compensating for her weight, so Brian could handle her quickly. She measured, absurdly, five and a half feet long. She functioned at bullet, laser speed, a contortionist and ballet dancer in one (large) rapier. She was black as midnight. Her hilt was elongated. The guard, also lengthy and the blade, edged on both sides—a formidable weapon. Her mind was at the center of the sword. The sword's mind was a total magical mystery. Her fuller and the flat acted if a slap, smack, whack or a good, solid spanking, were required. In the pommel itself, blessed on Lizardania and her own Black World, held most of her splendid mind.

Brian learned that size of mind wasn't important. It was the *concentration* of the mind; how much mind, regardless of size, revealed intelligence. The only way to kill this sword was to dissever the mind from the body. And if you've ever known, I mean really known, a Black World sword, you too would sell your life for it, and at a pin's fee!

FOUR

WARRING SAURIANS

"You have to be determined to change the world with your film, even though nothing changes."
—Hayao Miyazaki

All left save Littorian.

–That was a good explanation. They heard it, despite the damaged parts of your mind getting in the way.

–My mediocre brain was under some stress. You know I'm responsible.

–That's for you to decide, but you're not guilty. You couldn't have done anything for them. Their fate, well, was sealed.

–Can revenge bring them some peace?

–It won't have them rest any easier, my human friend.

–I'm sorry. Genotdelian wanted to destroy you, Littorian. He failed. Then he lashed out at us all.

–He will die for this. Anyone who has a mission is an angel. You've got to know that.

–Die?

–Yes. Genotdelian, Lord of the Crocodilians, will die.

–Are you going to kill him?

–As sure as you've got blood in your veins.

–Then, I'm going with you.

–No, you're not.

–Listen, I know you can stop me—well, duh. But please let me go.

–No.

–Please. I know where he's going.

Littorian, caught short, didn't know. And that was strange. Brian had his defenses up. He felt Littorian's presence. Littorian sighed.

–I see you've got your mental screens up. Formidable, seeing as how I taught you—but, no matter! He'll go to his home world. And that is all. There is no need for me to look inside you.

–Then you'll 'look' there in vain.

Littorian then frowned.

–I see. You tell me.

–Nothing doing.

–I'll just have to rip it out of your mind.

–Take me with you.

Littorian bent down. He squeezed Brian in his arms. But it was a loving squeeze.

–I can't let you be destroyed. I won't allow it—and by 'violence' or whatever that dick Death Incarnate said. The screwball's a trifle. He's a trifle to me! But still. He's not a trifle to you. I'd prefer you here, under Larascena and Clareina's care.

–I'll have my vengeance with Genotdelian. He deceived me— not you, Littorian. I've got 30 dates with him.

Littorian sighed, and heavily.

–Oh, alright. He deceived me too. And that's not fitting for a god.

–He's on Triton. And he's waiting.

–And on Triton he will die! My sword and weapons stay here.

Littorian was preparing to leave the *Echo.* The starship launched from Earth and was around Triton, all in a snap of mega-thrusters-and-minutes. This was as far as Brian could bring Littorian. At that moment, Littorian needed to lay down the law with Brian. Littorian knew he was tricky and wily. He needed to be short and firm.

—Stay here.

—But I want to go with you.

—You are kidding, right now, right? You'll get killed. That will get us *both* killed. You're supposed to bring my body home, and Larascena can make me well again. We agreed to that on the way out here. So don't worry, 'k? My Man, you'll see to that?

The Man turned towards the saurian. He was the co-pilot. The android's dark eyes flashed.

—I will see to it, my lord.

—Littorian, you have to survive.

—I can't count on that, my friend Brian. Genotdelian is, and I guess I can tell you this now, he's the serpent in your Bible. I think that's obvious now.

—I know.

—Huh?

—Tiperia told me.

—Oh, I see. No secrets now, eh? All my secrets lay on the table before my human. I guess that's fitting. I'm sorry Genotdelian was so 'inhumanly' cruel to you. Really, I am.

—It's alright—there wasn't anything you or I could do about that. I knew it had to be one of you. You know, to be the serpent.

Littorian was amused and let out a slight chuckle.

—I'm glad it wasn't me. I'd play a poor serpent, really. They're tricky, that's true, and I'm sure Genotdelian showed you some of that, but that Croc's got no sense of humor. There can be no heroes when dealing with gods whose one thought is vengeance. The greatest gift of the gods is raw, unmitigated power. My Man, watch Brian, he's tricky, in a good kinda way.

—But where on Triton do you wish to be let off?

Littorian just dismissed Brian and waved a taloned hand at the thought.

–We are 500 or 600 miles above the little moon now, right? This is sufficient. Again, stay here, I want you safe.

–I will find you, Littorian.

–I know you will. Be safe.

The door to the cabin closed. Immediately, the air was let out of the bay of the craft. Then it sealed itself back up. Littorian was gone.

Genotdelian suddenly appeared, coming around Neptune, at full force. He was a dragon, but more than just a dragon. Fat lived only in the dictionary. Twelve colossal abdominals, arms that would put Apollo to shame, the overall body could make the masses shrink down and beg for their lives. His wings, full of myriad muscles, stretched for miles and miles.

WHERE IS HE? WHERE, BRIAN MILLER? MY ONE CONCERN BEFORE I SEND YOUR PLANET, THE EARTH, INTO ASHES!

The Lord of the Lizardanians came on quickly, around Triton's northern tip. And on the largest moon of Neptune, Littorian and Genotdelian fought. Triton was about three quarters the size of the Earth's moon—but the saurians left it a jigsaw sliver. It reminded Brian of a Halloween pumpkin, with diagonal grooves cut out for a mouth. Half the moon was just blown away. The metal, below the surface of Triton, formed a molten film on the edges.

The star dragons bolted out rings of fire that nothing could resist. The sun was distant; the temperature on the moon was a startling two hundred plus below zero. That didn't concern the gods, though. Littorian used the moon as a shield between Genotdelian's great streams of fire. The planet's metal was turned red hot, turning to liquid and then fused away, against the terrific ropes of flames.

Brian put his (convenient) double-blinders on. Littorian went after Genotdelian. Littorian was so fixed on capturing his head, and then crushing it expertly, he thought of nothing else.

The two saurians grew to stretch for miles. Brian sitting in the command chair of the craft could see why he wasn't involved. They fought as the gods would fight—talons, sweeping tail swipes, and their incredible jaws pounding away at each other's scales. The jaws, wider than a football field, were increasingly bloody with every passing minute. Triton, which would normally stand idly by, was sliced and on fire. Genotdelian swept his tail and pieces came off of Triton like any dismembered birthday cake. Littorian swept it back, the sweeping, Triton rocks, by mental force, until the Crocodilian was covered with rock and metal. Littorian avoided the fires of the Lord of Crocodilia, by hiding around the moon. Littorian fought back with his own fire—green fire—so hot, it almost melted space itself.

–Are the shieldings on full power?

–They are, Brian. And they are buckling, the heat is too intense.

–Aren't we far enough away?

–If we want to survive, we have to get to Neptune's darker side, then come back. After it's over, I'm afraid. The Echo can do nothing to help Littorian.

–But we can't see anything, then!

The Man knew the stakes.

–We'll monitor them. Then we'll know when to come back.

–Nuh, let's stay so I can see; increase visibility to the maximum!

The fight went on for about an hour. Triton was devastated. Used as a shield, Littorian and Genotdelian set everything into embers. After a while, attentive people on Earth could see a pale light, shining in space.

The *Echo* was having problems. The Man became worried.

–Space itself is becoming unstable.

–Unstable. Define that for my 'tarded self.

–Space—they are warping space!

–How far does that spread?

–Maybe halfway to the next planet. This is the pattern of the gods. We have to get farther out.

The *Echo* continued to back up. Space stabilized at some distance from Neptune.

The furious beasts, spouting flames, locked arms around each other, snapping and biting. The craft began to shake apart, from their powerful grappling.

–Stay here, I've got to see…

The battle was going badly for Genotdelian. His body lay in crumples before the powerful Lizardanian. Genotdelian's wings were like wisps. He'd given his all, but Littorian still floated in, on strong, star dragon wings, for another rope-filled fire-patterned pass.

Genotdelian looked longingly at the *Echo*. While hundreds of miles out, he saw it with his keen eyes.

If I have to go, I'll make Littorian pay. I'll take the Echo—and that damn Brian Miller—with me!

Genotdelian rose strongly into space. He bulged out a belt of blazing power toward the *Echo*. Everything he had in his megaton lungs, a fire so strong, nothing could resist it.

–Oh, geez! All power to the shieldings *Echo*! Get us out of here!

The *Echo* applied all power to the shieldings—in vain. The *Echo* was halfway out of the effective range of Genotdelian's conflagration. The *Echo*, despite everything, was charbroiled in a bonfire.

Littorian boomed across space.

–NNNNOOOOOO!!!!

Littorian send a green-essence-blaze toward Genotdelian. The Crocodilian Warlord knew it was over. But he smiled as his soul came to an end—at least Brian Miller was no more.

Littorian, wings blazing, grabbed the cindered outline of Genotdelian and crushed him to nothingness. Then, he swung over to the burned-out *Echo*, and rose to the distant Earth, cradling the forlornness in his massive chest. The time it took was instant, far beyond light speed.

Littorian ended up looking at Larascena with a profundity she never saw on a saurian. Larascena seemed to be taken aback. Then, realization hit.

—Save him!

Larascena went to work immediately. A table was set up, magically. The *Echo* was separated from the crisp corpse, with her talented claws. Larascena went into her healing mode on the body.

—Help me, Littorian!

The Lord of the Lizardanians, shrunk down to his eight feet size, his strong wings a forgotten memory, helped Larascena with a hand over hers. The unrestrained recuperative power was overwhelming. All the other saurians were backed up, in awe. Brian Miller was coming back. His skeleton, skin and muscle all came back in a flash. But something was holding him back. The something holding Brian back was something no saurian, anywhere, could ever dissever. It had to be confronted.

Larascena was flustered, and picked Brian up in her claws, shaking him back and forth like a rabbit.

—There is nothing physically wrong with him, Littorian! Oh, this stupid human. Getting smoldered with Crocodilian fire!

—You know <u>what</u> it is, Larascena. I'm going into his mind.

—Oh, no. Brian's promise to Death Incarnate, that's it! This was by violence, just as He predicted.

Littorian put a hand on Larascena, indicating to stop shaking Brian before the human's teeth fell out.

—Not while I'm around!

In a moment, Littorian entered Brian's mind, and was gone.

Littorian appeared before Death Incarnate.

—Well, look who's here! It's the Lord of the Lizardanians. I was expecting, maybe the Alligatorian Warlord Larascena? You knew about Brian's little promise to me? So this is the "companion level of trust," I see. This is Death's Doorstep, and you've never been here before? A son of God appearing before me, is that correct? His life is mine, now. Clear out, unless you want to feel my scythe on your handsome neck! Or is it distressing to hear an ancient relic talking about your fine, and very vital, handsomeness this way?

–It's you that should 'clear out,' Death Incarnate.

–And what's all that supposed to mean? This is where I'm God!

–I don't have any quarrel with you. I have no chess pieces to play you a game.

–What would be the stakes of our little chess game? Goodness me, I've already won! Good to know you don't have a quarrel with me, though. The companion stays with me. That was our bargain. All the rest is silence, in this senseless terror, that is life. You are on Death's Doorstep and here, there is darkness and there is no one to listen to your lament. Indifference is reflected on you, oh saurian, by indifference from God. I'm here to *collect,* as per our agreement. You've no place here!

–No, that was *your* bargain, your *agreement. I* had nothing to do with that—hence Brian is, ergo, coming with me.

Littorian ripped Brian out of Death Incarnate's grip.

–Brian's mine, saurian! When my scythe falls, nothing can stop it. His soul is *mine!*

His scythe was raised and was falling. Nothing could stop it. Nothing. Brian, in Littorian's arms, could not. Littorian looked up at the scythe. Littorian still had hope; and hope was all he needed to have. That would be enough.

Then, the scythe met a force. It was not the neck of Brian Miller. It was a power the scythe did not recognize. Death Incarnate was astounded, and that hadn't happened in many an age and a night. Michael, the Archangel, with his sword, blocked the scythe of Death Incarnate. The sword, blue and white, got in the way of the scythe's sharpened point.

–Go. I'll hold them off. Just go. Brian's life has not fled from his body, his soul is still there! Run, Littorian, in your mind, and *his*, to Earth!

–Thank you, Michael.

–It's been a long time, since we were together.

Death Incarnate saw what was happening. He couldn't believe it.

–Michael, the Archangel, what are you doing here? This is Death's doorstep. Do you even know where you are? And aren't you supposed to smite the serpent, Michael? Isn't this your opportunity?

–This isn't the serpent; this *is* my brother. No burden is he. His welfare, that's <u>my</u> main concern. Am I not my brother's keeper? It was Littorian that smote the serpent and saved *me* the trouble! My brother cannot encumber me. Go, Littorian, and I will hold them here.

Death Incarnate laughed incredulously.

–You'll hold *what* here? I am the Unknown! I am the Unknowing! You'll hold what here!?! You cannot 'hold' Death anywhere! You cannot hold Death Incarnate! And where is God? Is it time for Him to come to me? You can't hold me!

–No, I can't. But I <u>can</u> hold your scythe. Just go, Littorian!

Littorian swung in the air, in full dragon form, holding Brian Miller, and disappeared.

–Brian? Are you okay?

Brian saw Littorian's concerned face.

–Wow. I remember telling *Echo* to veer away from Genotdelian. Uh, did he make it?

Littorian just did his characteristic wiggle-of-head and looked at Larascena. Larascena picked Brian up and hugged him, sincerely. Brian's body was squeezed to the point of popping against her mighty, maximized chest.

–Okay…geez, you're breaking me, now! I'm only, *only* human!

–Oh, fragile teenager.

Larascena reluctantly set him down.

–It's good to get you back. You witnessed the gods fighting? Not the place to be. I wish I'd been there *just* to haul you away. Then my sword can give you a good spanking.

Littorian then looked down. He healed himself but didn't want to describe his injuries. But they were substantial.

–Genotdelian is no more. I killed his soul. I really didn't approve of his reign. Enough said.

–But Littorian, hey! What happened afterwards? I confess, I don't remember it!

–Sometimes you can have dreams, in that state, you know? It's probably just a dream. Anyway, it was nothing a god can't handle, my friend. Put it down as a 'good angel experience,' alright? I think Soreidian has something to say to me. Excuse me; Larascena, I leave Brian in your care. Of The Man and *Echo*, I will see to them later. No liaisons, both of you.

–Ah! Easy for you to say, my Lord of the Lizardanians!

–I know he's safe with you, Lara.

Soreidian's team, sitting Sphinx-like, saw everything. Larascena and Littorian saved Brian Miller—and it was so much of a sin, Soreidian couldn't put it into words.

Soreidian left the group and stood apart, waiting for Littorian. The Lord of the Lizardanians walked casually over, his long tail, an inch from the ground.

–You summoned me, Soreidian? I see your team was of no help whatever. What do you want?

Soreidian appeared grave and spoke only in a whisper. More than mere words were communicated between the saurians. At evidence, was the extreme and totally unforgiveable sin of grabbing Brian's soul standing at the Gate of Death. That had never happened before. Curing was fine, and even after death—but once Death Incarnate had someone's soul—that was it. Littorian must step down as Lord of the Lizardanians.

Littorian heard Soreidian out. Soreidian stood about nine-feet high and was a Lizardanian of some note. Littorian was just eight-feet tall and had to look up to meet the eyes of Soreidian. His second destroyed one of the top Crocodilians on Earth, Heritian. He had a conscience when it came to humans now, especially Russian humans. That was another reason he wanted to escape the confines of Earth, to escape the Russians. Littorian saw things a bit differently, in accord with Brian's wishes. Soreidian respected that Littorian had killed the Lord of Crocodilia, but he set that aside.

–My lord, this cannot go on. The Companionship is broken before you. The humans, well, they can't handle us. If you get a Crocodilian down to Earth, just one, he'll incinerate anything and everything. The human's nuclear toys and whatever else they have now won't end a Croc. Even a hydrogen bomb or a neutron bomb or whatever else they have (now), will just make a Croc mad. It would take more firepower to end one, as you know.

–Hey, I like the pun.

–Punning's not in order here. It definitely shows that you're young, after what you've done to Brian. Just give the order to go, to *Tiperia* and all saurians. And we won't speak of it again.

–Give the order? Huh? I'll give no such 'orders,' Soreidian. If *you* want to go, then go. Abandon the humans to the Crocodilians? Not yet, I think. The Crocodilians haven't chosen a leader—they need the time to do it. I've thought to them. I await a message back. Now, we could have peace between saurians, everywhere. That's something to wait for, I think—and then, we can go.

–I'm getting everyone together for a Hearing, my lord. And we will discuss what you've done to Brian. That was a violation. I'm recommending a trial.

–A what? You will? You, oh, you just do what you want to do. Silly saurian, you're just such a fruit loop.

–I see you've learned something of language from our little companion.

–I know not to say you're trying to build a bicycle while riding it. But you are, you know.

–Our laws are a mystery to you, my Lord Littorian.

–And so they will remain a mystery. I embrace anarchy; strange that you do not?

Soreidian left, in something of a huff. Littorian just dismissed it. Brian Miller watched his conversation, with crossed arms. Littorian walked back to him, with a grin. Brian knew it was a grin, because it exceeded the 'smile lines' cascading across Littorian's face.

—I think you and I are due for a trip, Brian. I've got to see my home again. I thought to all our friends before I left. The Seree were the first to arrive. It's the *Mixcoatl* and captain Grendel. That was played upon by Genotdelian. He mixed up all the signals, which had me confused. It was a tragic error. I regret it, but I don't regret us. We should rebuild that Companion Program.

—I'm looking forward to seeing the Seree again and it'll be my first time in Lizardania. Hey, what did Soreidian say?

—Huh? My local, *da fuq* space cadet? Oh, my human, I blew him off. I'm not waiting on tender hooks to talk to him again. He's kinda crazy, you know. I think it's spending all his free time with the Russians. I understand they are fond of drink, yes?

—Yeah, Vodka and the like. I wonder if he's had his adventitious 'toddy' today already. What effect will alcohol have on a Lizardanian?

—I'm afraid that it will have an effect. A toddy? Such strange expressions, you have; it's not like I'm picking up any such things from listening to humans, you know. We'll have to get him a bale or a bottle or a bushel or whatever it comes in, right? That's what you call being drunk, correct? I'd like to see him snookered, just once. All Vodka corrupts, but Absolut vodka corrupts—for absolutely sure!

FIVE

JOAN OF ARC REBORN

[But she said], where d'you wanna go?
How much you wanna risk?
I'm not looking for somebody
With some superhuman gifts
Some superhero
Some fairytale bliss
Just something I can turn to
Somebody I can kiss...
<u>Something Just Like This</u>, by The Chainsmokers
& Coldplay

I arrived at Joan of Arc's mini-mini castle at our camp in the Everglades. Soon enough, the outpost would go to human hands. That wasn't just good, that was the best! The castle was attached on the main house by a quaint, little drawbridge. The totally enterprising Black World weapons had constructed it all for Joan, out of French mortar and bricks making it look like a castle from the 1400s. Anything and everything to make Joan feel more at home.

I opened the medieval door (cleverly Black World weapon-designed) and, refreshingly, light music was playing. It was time to draft another leader, a better leader to the *new* 30 Companions. I was really looking forward to it, I'd speak to Jeanette directly. I had a grocery bag in my hands, just to make a subtle point with Jeanne. Wasn't too sure how much The Maid was up on global-warming. That's a chance I had to take. A danger I'm prepared to face. ...but then Joan was dancing around, and, damn, around, I thought she was raving drunk as a lady-lord! Her hair was a massive-blond-genius, tingling-down-and-richly-down, almost to the marble floor. 'Bob' haircut be damned, I guess. She was singing along with Karen Carpenter and the song was "Close To You," and she was prancing everywhere with flower petals galore, sprinkling-anyhow, singing pleasantly:

Why do birds suddenly appear?
Every time, you are near?
Just like me, they long to be, close to you!

I thought about Karen's life, feeling that Jeannette had no idea about how she tragically ended. That was good, I didn't feel like being a cloud over Joan of Arc, dragging her down. Me? I wanted to raise her up, gloriously. I gently closed the door, saving the surrender of the 30 companions for another time, and face to face with Korillia! I swallowed asphalt, forcing my smile.

–Oh, glad to see you, my lady. I know your intention is to see Jeannette, but this global warming thing has me really concerned, and I think the Wysterian could use your help and I also think—

As usual, she just blew me off, with the trivial hand gesture, making those seven-inch claws come uncomfortably close to my face. I didn't back up, so assured was I with her grace. Naturally, I trusted her completely.

–Ah, not to worry my silly Terran, Teresian has that on her list, forget this 'warming' stuff and concentrate on leaving this whore

Earth or I will take you away myself. This is just a product of your shitty environment, what else is new? Clareina and Larascena will thank me for taking you away from Earth. Are you blocking that door, so I can't get to *L'alouette*, my little Jeanne d'Arc? This, like all human stuff, has gone on too long. As you know, the end of this new beginning is near. How do you feel?

—In your presence, my lady, I feel fine. It's only been a few months, that we've come to know saurians, how does that compare to someone who has lived eons, like you? Like people down South say, "Let the slick end slide and the rough end drag," right?

—Going to let me by, or do I have to get rough?

—Please. Just look at this rough-and-miscellaneous grocery bag, oh, it's alright if you take it, I know you're a dragon star and would take it anyway. It's just a for-instance, speaking of global warming, a bag you'd get at the supermarket. First, as you see, it's light brown paper, not plastic, so it's not like contributing to the plastic-lakes in the oceans. I understand the Black World Swords are doing something about that as a <u>favor</u> for the new 30 companions, and that's great. Look at this, the bag has got the weight, in pounds, that it can hold, well, six pounds! And it's got the makers of the bag on the side of it, three people made this bag, see their names? And it was made in the USA, you see, giving jobs to those people, and perhaps more. It's got a serial number on it, and the renewable, recyclable and sustainable stuff on there, too. I know I'm being quite forward with you now, Korillia. I think Global Warming is a real concern and I'm bold enough to talk about whatever it is, even without substantial information or the facts. The scientists got it figured out, so I look to them. It contains a minimum (hear that, a minimum!) of 40% post-consumer material already! It's almost recyclable now, what do you think, my lady and heir apparent Warlord of Lizardania, Korillia?

Korillia's permanent smile went down as I concluded my little speech. That's hard to do, if your born a star dragon. I needed her to smile more, not less. She took the bag from my hand. Of a bigly-sudden, she punched through the bag, with her mighty-duke (no big deal there) but then the reptilian crushed up the bag and put her condensed fist, inches from my face, and really crunched it down, vibrating slightly. The Lizardanian crushed the paper to miniature-nothing, with a hand that could level any mountain, her 50-plus-inch biceps erupting, pouting and pulsing. Korillia revealed her sleek, scaled palm, the slightest dust, which she proceeded to blow in my astounded mug.

–There. Now I've cured this global warming myself, with your little bag. Yes, scientist know a lot, right, like bleeding people, and taking cadavers and drinking their blood, and now you believe in what they are telling you today, or yesterday?

Strangely, even with this miniscule-power display, I felt more comfortable with being with the saurians every day, such feats of strength notwithstanding. Maybe this was just the "emerging dragon" in me, just trying to be at home, change is life's nature and it's hope.

–What other favors have you got, my little human nizzle?

–I think getting out of this conversation is my best course, my lady.

Korillia departed with a little dragon-esque flourish, darting her city-and-county-smashing fingers around, benignly of course, skimming by me.

–It seems so, concern yourself with our leaving procedures so we can finally get going, I was just about to tell Joan of Arc myself!

After the very epic football game, Jeanette managed that very fatal predilection given to some teenagers: *Thinking.* She could see the whole world, the one in the 1400s and today. How little mankind had advanced, how very little, so few noble and fallacious thoughts were present now-days. This was not 'new' (and nothing is, under the sun) but the very concept of 'companionship' in this sense (and I say that with real emphasis) was something modern. That's what Joan thought about, another race 'got something' out of companionship, needed the advice of humanity, young advice.

Of Tiperia, that Starfinder considered the general plan, in retrospect. The actions on that football field were designed to wear-out the saurians in a passionate game. All this was orchestrated by Tiperia. She loved Littorian, knowing the situation very well. The secret was Joan. Tiperia knew of Soreidian's might, something so powerful, humans could be swept up and *kaput-ted*. Human beings could be so intricate, so profound, and could love-so-endlessly. The Starfinder also knew that love was strong, but love didn't have any antitank guns, grenades, missiles, mortars, nuclear weapons, airplanes, and all those war-weapons that was the *real-politick* of modern times. She wanted to preserve the companion program, the teenagers guiding the anarchist saurians, but how to keep Soreidian and Littorian from killing each other over it all? Joan of Arc offered her a way out.

Jeannette had some crazy religious ways. Tiperia respected those ideas, too. Thesis, Antithesis and eventually Synthesis, good building blocks to infuse in Joan. Then, learning that, she would see how you have to <u>change</u> (or modify) your ideas given time. And that time-infinity Tiperia did have. Even 'truth' could be measured given time, and human understanding must reach a 'new' Synthesis, change is constant, you had to be flexible in your thinking. Remember, even here, power can 'create' truth (but can it maintain it, forever?). Truth is limited, that's the indictment of truth. So non-power can create non-truth in the minds of the people. People are like fish, all grouped together, lemmings to the world and if everyone declares it to be truth, then it's that way. Only later do you see what fools humanity always is, and probably, was. Saying there is no 'later' doesn't make it so. There is a 'later,' the double-indictment of mankind. Tiperia had one weakness, however: She loved Littorian. He was so infinitely strong, he could love her, *her way*, and far, far over it. So Littorian must be preserved. Soreidian was a Lizardanian, and hated Brian Miller. The Starfinder applied her secret hope: Joan of Arc.

Happy it was all over and happier too that the leading saurians were completely exhausted, Joan of Arc had a victory celebration with Tiperia—sort of. The god was pleased, Joan had saved Tiperia's lover.

–Anything you want, Jeanne la Pucelle, you ask, and I will bend Space, Time and Distance, my episodic and nemesis Trinity and it's all yours, come, what do you need from me? The fact that you and Dracula have a year together, well, I conclude that's just coincidence. Coincidences do exist, but they are rare, still, I'm of the opinion that they happen. However, thesis, antithesis and synthesis, right? It's just a pack of little white lies (that is thesis and antithesis fighting it out) building up to our 'bigger' synthesis, the bigger 'justified' truth. For now, that's the truth. Later, it will become a lie, too, after it breaks down with thesis and antithesis, okay? I claim the right to change my mind, as any good woman should. That is the universal Right of Woman, *to change her mind*. So, again, your desires? –I'm sure your aware of my yearning to rescue the Donner Party. Let me take a temporary rain check on my wish, perhaps I will need it later on. I'd like to guide my own companion, my lady, and that's all you can do for me. If the Donner Party comes, it comes! If it turns out to be their time, it's their time.

Tiperia smiled.

Teresian, the Wysterian, her brother Kukulkan, together with a revitalized Littorian and I, Brian Miller, had a talk about the favors granted to the humans by the dragons. Thing was, 30 'favors' for 30 companions. I didn't even argue with these three dragon-stars about their 'dissipation' of the favors, and everyone just lost track of them anyway. Of course! They are anarchists, and 'saying' there were 30 favors didn't influence them one way or the other. In addition, wildfires were a thing of the past, too, with Crocodilians on-call. They were very skilled at setting up conflagrations outside of fire-starters, burning them out that way. This was considered a pleasantry on the diplomatic side, but in secret, the Crocodilians loved fire.

In addition, Teresian put the Black World weapons on the idea of 'curing the common cold,' as one of the favors for the 30 companions. The Wysterians both felt grieved over the death of the original 30 companions during the harsh reign of Genotdelian, the late Lord of the Crocodilians, as did his successor, Turinian. In one humorous exchange, they believed that 60 favors should be granted to humanity, with another 30 piled on as an apology. Those 30 killed companions had family members, and shouldn't they be 'granted' favors? Counting, say, four family members apiece, shouldn't they receive 120 favors? Giving the humans something, they want everything. What about great grandparents, uncles, aunts, half-brothers, half-sisters, and all of that mankind-action? When this conversation got up to the thousands of favors, I knew it was time to bring it to a polite end. Cures to coronavirus, various forms of influenza (and everything so derived in the Spanish flu of 1918), kidney problems, smallpox, Ebola virus, rabies, AIDS-HIV, Hantavirus, Cocoliztli, Dengue, Rotavirus, SARS, MERS, diphtheria, all kinds of plagues, they just took the whole medical book and made cures for everything and 'gave it all' to the medical community, closing the world-wide human medical book with a Black-World harrumph. The weapons really wanted a challenge. Look at the human DNA and the juvenile replicating of RNA, had the weapons looking skyward saying "That's all you've got, bitch?" The battle was over in a day and a half. Going further down the list, all the sexual diseases in the nasty, sordid human repertoire were countenanced, too. And after that, 'dealing with' Skid Row and the worst cities in the world without bloodshed, was on tap. That was if (and only if) the dragons could stay around. Afterall, the Black World weapons needed something to do.

What the medical community did with these cures was another affair. Some thought all the viruses were acts of the military, for keeping people in line. The Black World weapons all agreed with the saurian design for leaving humans to figure out humans, they were for departing soon.

Meanwhile, the Alligatorian Warlord was watching a movie as a 'last call on Earth' in my office, so I interrupted her.

–Whatja watching, Lara?

–It's *The Lair of the White Worm*, by Bram Stoker, but I'm guessing it's a—what do you call it? A comedy, maybe? You know I don't believe in religion, or the Masons, Illuminati, Scientology, EST, and everything and anything human at all, it's all just associations and contacts, all of it. Damn you humans are boring. You simians can't be alone, hence religion. However, I do believe in you, Brian. As to the movie, the fangs are cool. Strange that the bad guys don't have the ultra-strength of real serpents, too bad. Come and watch, find a spot next to me, right there, good, it's a funny movie, enjoy it with me.

–Sure! Sure I will. Say, I was interested in going to Iran with Littorian, just for a visit before we all leave. Can you and Clare accompany us?

–Yeah, I'll go, uh-huh. I'm just following the white dragon on your arm; just watch this movie and let your hands be very liberal, mine back! Next I'm going to watch *King Kong vs. Godzilla*, the humans filmed this in 1962, should be fun!

–My lady let's skip out on that one. Hey, let's us watch *Godzilla vs. Kong*, that'll be much better. Wouldn't want you to enflame Japan, or any-such-thing. I had more than my share of that with Danillia. Besides, you might not like how that 1962 one turns out. In the meantime, for *The Lair*, let my liberalities begin!

SIX

SEARCHING FOR SAURIAN PARENTS-IN-LAW(LESS)

Brian set off to find the parents of the Warlord. Clareina's parentages couldn't be found, not so Larascena. He left his pre-wives sleeping on the grass, a sudden liaison's benign aftermath. It was an effort, Brian felt drained, in a spirited way. The human felt this was the right time to see Larascena's parents. He was really woozy, but after a quick shower, going back to the guest castle, he felt refreshed.

He felt like getting drunk, but a session with the twin-saurians sent his mind and body skyward. Strangely, the parents were absent during their arrival on Crocodilia. His female Black sword was concerned and gripped his shirt with her guard. Playfully he caressed her.

–You okay, thinking of bringing me with?

–Nah. Just stay here. Play with your pre-husband. I'm sure he needs you as much as I needed my sleeping pre-wives (ahem).

–You'll regret it. These Alligatorians can't burn you, and that's a blessing. However, they can do magic. Oh, well, don't worry; I'll just look around for a hands-in-his-pockets toad, after, with a sex-starved grin.

That stung, and Brian hesitated.

–The knives and the hatchets are all having fun now, it's safe, and I gave them the day off.

–Least someone's having fun. I should be off with my man, Larascena's sword. But I'm not. I'm with you. He's planning the wedding alone.

–I have to meet Larascena's parents first.

–You'll regret it, jes' sayin'.

Brian then hugged his Black World sword. Her blades weren't sharp, just to compensate. She sighed, in his arms.

–Now you're just being silly. You take too many chances, my human.

–Around you, I always have a chance. 'Silly' around you is okay, right, my Black sword?

–Too bad I can't marry you, too.

–What? We aren't married now?

She hugged him back, strongly. The female sword could crush him in her extended guards, but loved him, wanted Brian to be safe. She knew he was only a kid, only a child. She'd lived a long life, evidenced by her scars and pieces missing off her shoulder, fuller and guard, and she knew the sacrifice Brian had gone through for the hatchet. She decided that needed a mention.

–I appreciate your cost for the hatchets, that fee was too high, but you did it anyway. Now that hatchet has found love, and that's romantic. You certainly increased your loyalty quotient, doing that for your male hatchet.

–Oh shucks, ma'am.

–Yeah. Strain yourself <u>not</u> to be funny. About these Alligatorians, I know they're supposed to be friendly, slated to be your parents-in-law and all but...

–Alright, don't go on, just stand by me, on my hip.

–Not on your back?

—Nah, I just don't want to seem too aggressive. It'll be okay.

—As though being on my hip is not as aggressive as being on your back?

—Don't get so particular.

The sword didn't say anything. Didn't think anything. Just took a position on Brian's hip with a barely audible sigh.

After the conversation with his sword, Littorian was worried, too.

—Want me to go with you?

—Geez, everyone's so paranoid. Doesn't my diplomacy have any play at all, my lord?

—I don't want to be too helicoptery around you; but I am concerned.

—They'd have to get rid of Larascena sometime, isn't it better with me?

—Yes, but don't use that argument with them—you'd lose your head, literally.

Brian just gave Littorian a hug, as was his wont, then went out of the City Guest Building, looking up the street. He had reports from the weapons concerning Medeian and Demeterian. Larascena, by now awake, on her floor, was still making demands about the appearance and architecture to legion female Crocodilians. Later that day, everyone would have to move out of the building because the 'floor,' was not tall enough to support her wild visions. Brian didn't want to bother her. Besides, he considered he'd have to 'man-up,' on something, not just to impress Larascena (that couldn't be done, anyway), but just to prove he wasn't a *girly-girl*.

He approached the building, which was more like a castle, than anything else.

Two Crocodilians stood in the doorway, and these were the biggest they had, at well over 18 feet high, a pillar of strength. At this height, their arms where more like *broad* doors, (multiple doors) they were that thick. They were mountainous giants compared to the solitary human. Since peace was at hand, Brian just came right up to them. Brian was ready to talk in Crocodilian.

–My honored and deviated Crocodilians, greeting at you. You have two Alligatorians in you. Can please I speak to these?

The Crocodilians shook their heads awkwardly, the bad Crocodilian washing over them. Lucky for Brian, they were briefed on his arrival.

–Let's just talk in Universalian, my young human. So. You plan to marry the Warlord of Alligatoria, and, by rumor, a Lizardanian, too?

–Yes, my lord, I do.

–Sure, you can enter. The parents are on the third floor. It's Demeterian and Medeian, and, uh, enter at your own risk, of course.

That last comment so grated the sword, she jacked up her pommel up about two inches, right against Brian's forearm. She said nothing, thought nothing. Brian did a double take, then eyed the giant saurians' suspiciously, and blew it off. Brian responded in Universalian.

–Thanks, I guess. I'm sure everything will be alright.

The 18 footers exchanged a quizzical look, and smirked. He entered the house and proceeded up the stairs. The building only had five floors, and he thought he'd better walk it.

He arrived on the third floor. The room was all in marble, floor to ceiling. Brian saw two Alligatorians talking quietly.

–Hi, I'm Brian Miller, pleased to meet you, and can we—oh... oh, shi—

Demeterian cut Brian off, seemingly literally.

–You shaddap, you ameba, you frickin' interloper! This human is playing rooster to our hen Larascena, my husband! I'm not going to allow this human to shake any saurian chick, getting his short-dick fuck on. It'd take only 283-foot pounds of pressure to crush your skull in. That's a pittance to a saurian. <u>Do</u> ask me of a pittance, you chimpanzee-mannequin!

Demeterian was in the air, like a giant wasp-snake, teeth gnashing, when her husband belted out.

–I'll reach down and pull his camel hump outta his mouth; I'll squash his scrotum like any alien pancake, lemme at this apish simian! I'll make a yawning tragedy out of your fool monkey face!

This was definitely a surprise to Brian Miller, these feelings from his would-be-parents-in-law. They were very 'handsome,' people. Brian was keen on looking at saurians and could easily tell they were in the highest class of all Alligatoria. Brian could certainly see where Larascena got her looks from, and to see them in a rage, really depressed Brian. He thought the Black weapons would give those grapevine rumors of his good deeds, of saving Larascena, the Warlord, and the soul of the hatchet, but not so. Their reaction wasn't the scary thing, not at all.

It was the wings.

The segments on their prodigious backs, jutting those massive pinions, defying and destroying the room all to pieces, throwing steel and cement (or the Crocodilian equivalent thereof) everywhere and anywhere, had Brian cringing, drawing back. He reached for his Black sword but found it already in his hand. It was doing defense against the four knives and four hatchets all intend on making ribbons out of Brian's throat, flying at him. The defined, muscled soaring power of a star dragon, scales throughout, pulsing strength that could overthrow a whole building on a whim, with their puissant might, propelled Brian backwards. His sword was the one throwing him back. She was prepared and already was counting on a frontal attack by the other Black weapons. The Black World swords, she thanked the gods, were still in the colossal hands of the saurians.

The window didn't matter to the seasoned Black sword. Nothing could or would touch Brian. To someone unseen, Brian flying 40 feet above the earth holding on to his blade, the female sword screamed aloud.

–Hey, every other Black weapon, ho! Don't you know who this is? It's the human who got the hatchet's soul back! He saved Larascena. I know you've heard about it in thought!

She gave Brian a smooth ride down, underneath him like a surfboard, then she witched hands, to his right, with his two fingers up to her mind on the guard and pommel. The Black World sword was so prepared for this and very smooth about execution. In karate-pose, Brian's left hand raised up in a chop-mode.

Hey, put your hand on my grip, yes, both hands, unless you intent to lose it, right now. Those hatchets and knives will be looking for something like this; you with your sorrowful skin up against two saurians and vengeful weapons from my world, you <u>think</u> and correctly, too, lest I spank you!

Brian, still shocked that his sword was right about everything, put both hands on the grip, with <u>four fingers</u>, moved smoothly up, resting on her never-ending, superior mind.

The saurians landed heavily before Brian, two angry Alligatorian serpents, very pissed (over nothing), grown to gargantuan size at least as tall as the now decimated building crumbling behind them. Their many muscled wings over Brian's head, they shattered the whole building, just to get at him. They still had their swords in their scaled hands, and that's what Brian's sword was looking for. The swords grew along with their masters, too. The hatchets and knives, she could handle them. As soon as they landed on the ground, four hatchets and four knives surrounded them. They were under orders, the first of them to cut Brian's throat would be rewarded. Brian's sword caught some of the many Black weapons' thoughts all thrown around. What the 'reward' was, she didn't know. The star dragons, not caring about the mess around them, or the shocked look of the Crocodilian passers-by, or the guards, everyone at sixes-and-sevens, prepared to pounce with their swords upraised. The megaton muscles on their legs were fit to spring, their myriad teeth, and, in giant form, three feet long at least, were gnashing together. Brian noticed with some admiration their abdominal supremacy was totally maxed out, in an ultra-Herculean way. Now Brian knew were Larascena got those splendid structures, the DNA was palpable (and now, overwhelming). He cringed at meeting Clareina's parents—would they have been worse? They mercifully left Clareina on her own, indifferent to whom she married.

The call of Brian's female sword was heard. Multiple swords, knives and hatchets came over at warp speed, landing in front of Brian. His sword welcomed the assistance.

This is Brian Miller, the savior of the soul of the hatchet, from the Black World! Need (just a little) help.

Many weapons, including some from Littorian's Fellowship, were arriving too. Larascena's own sword showed up entirely pissed. The Warlord's sword immediately went up to "his woman," almost falling over himself to defend the female sword.

–WHAT IN THE BLUE BLAZES IS GOING ON OVER HERE! YOU TWO SWORDS, *YES YOU*, STAND DOWN IMMEDIATELY!

Then, Littorian's sword, assuming the 'eloquence' of the Lord of the Lizardanians sprang over everyone and had a <u>very</u> commanding voice.

–ARE YOU BAT SHIT CRAZY, ATTACKING THIS HUMAN? I'M LITTORIAN'S BLACK WORLD SWORD, STAND DOWN, YOU TWO PSYCHOS!

Medeian's sword, a female, hesitated, as did Demeterian's sword, a male. The commandeering voice from another Black sword had them at sixes and sevens. The weapons surrounding Brian now backed off. They couldn't get to Brian anyway; too many knives and hatchets were guarding him now. The group arrived, in a blaze of star dragon wings, beating about. With them were the human companions, everyone racing over.

Amazingly, the two star dragons, despite everything, pounced again on Brian Miller. Their teeth never broke through the line, set up like a World War One trench, heavily defended. Now, other saurians were holding them back, three to each one of them, all of them 'dragon sized' now, pushing them back. The building-length saurians from the Fellowship were only <u>barely</u> restraining the parents. The beating of the wings made a whirl wind, but Brian's sword set up a little, impenetrable sphere around Brian. His white hair didn't even fly out now. Brian just stood by in a pleasant wait, for everything and everyone to calm down. He waited too for the Godzilla-sized saurians to grow down to their normally intimidating selves.

Finally, Littorian then arrived with Larascena, in star dragon form, lamenting the destruction caused by the two rabid saurians. It was more embarrassing for Larascena because these were her parents. Brian, despite all the incredible destruction, was uninjured.

–Mother! Father! This is how you greet my pre-husband? In front of the Crocodilians you destroyed one of their buildings, set up to give you comfort? I'm ashamed to be an Alligatorian!

At that, Demeterian and Medeian cringed and (literally) shrunk down. Littorian, along with everyone else, just stayed silent (doing their own shrinking now). Larascena's charge was enough, no need to pile on.

Brian, with hands on his sword hilt, tried to put his hand down. He made an effort. Still, the hand stayed firmly fixed.

It's okay, my little femme fatale, we can relax; let's put our hands down now, right?

Nah-uh.

I'm kind of embarrassed right now, so please lower them.

Nah.

What's to worry about now? Everyone's around. This is some kind of a provocation.

Not 'til I'm sure they've settled down.

They're settled, see, they transformed now into eight feet legions of saurian tragic terror, so everything's alright?

Littorian and Larascena looked over and saw his hands shaking.

You're going to give me another stroke like this, and I don't want to end up like Lenin…but maybe that'd be good if you think—

The sword clanged out of his hands and hit the marble tile and it cracked. Everyone jumped at the noise. Brian didn't see that coming. He lost his footing, all very awkwardly.

Littorian then came over and put his claws lightly on Brian's shoulder, helping him up.

–Problems getting your sword to behave? It's good that she was so aware of the instincts of these saurians to their child. You should be thankful.

At least someone respects what I've done, huh!

–Yes, I'm thankful and have thought and said that to her.

Strange, I didn't hear anything, Brian? Still waiting.

Meanwhile, Larascena was talking to her parents in the most intense way. Medeian and Demeterian looked down at the marble floor, the part that wasn't decimated by them. Their wings put away, and reduced in size, they seemed embarrassed getting this heart-felt lecture by Larascena. The Fellowship, seeing all was calm again, just wandered off to the attentions of the Crocodilians, fluttering around them.

Larascena abruptly left the parents, standing off to one side. Magically, she righted everything that was wrong, the marble tiles fixed, the building repaired, the broken and uprooted trees surrounding the residence green again, everything and anything that her parents sent to Armageddon in talons and teeth. When done, Larascena looked quite a bit drained, but she didn't care. The Crocodilians were amazed that one Alligatorian could do so much fixing. Larascena then walked awkwardly over to Brian, clawing tenderly her own face.

–That had to be a little debilitating, Larascena.

–Lara, damn it, and I won't tell you that again. It was nothing, not to me. You okay?

–Sure, thanks to my sword, I never felt bett—

–Good, I'm done with you. Tomorrow we get this wedding ceremony over with—see you tonight. I'm sorry.

That, with a *tutt-tutt* with her claws, her many minions, hiding in doorways, ran over to her, notes in hand. She walked away with all of them nodding up and down in a wise, serpentine way, a dozen female Crocodilians at least, fragile blossoms (under notoriously strong scales), and laboriously writing things down about improving Larascena's living quarters.

Then, Brian stood alone with the parents. Both were fully armed though. They talked briefly together, sighed, and then came over to him. Brian's sword was leery, and hopped Brian away a good ten feet.

Hey, don't do that!

I'm in charge here, my stupid little human, and I've your pecker in check, and you'll do what I say.

Brian wisely demurred.

The two saurians stopped. Then, they dismissed their swords and other weapons. The weapons then flew off in the direction of Littorian's Fellowship.

I'll have to dismiss you too.

You try that I'll cause you to have that stroke, because then you'd be crazy.

Oh, just stay at my side. Stubborn sword.

Who just saved your life, yet again? Hyper-stupid human? That was a bravura performance, just now, and you know it!

Brian made ready with his best Alligatorian language.

–Let's try this again. I guess now I'm not coming in like a rainbow. Hi, there! I'm Brian Miller, and I'm ever so glad to meet you finally, my lord and lady, and, by Larascena's accounts, my pre-parents-in-law!

The two had a mocking look cross their scaled faces, and their teeth shone brightly. Their nostrils (or snouts, if you prefer) grew, just slightly. Both just sat down Sphinx-like. They could try to kill Brian again. Obviously, they promised Larascena that they wouldn't.

–I'm afraid I can't sit like that, so please you. We do have a companion with us that can. Her name is Jing Chang and she's from China, on Earth. I'd be happy to intro—

Medeian, very old, as was his wife, just waved a claw, simulating cutting Brian off.

–Let's speak in Universalian. I've pledged my life to see that you're safe, to Larascena. By the way, your Alligatorian language seems a little, uh, taxed.

Brian switched over to Universalian, with some relief.

—I'm against taxes, unless there's a <u>return</u> on them, and then it's just take that check to the bank, right?

—Huh?

—Never mind, just a human joke.

The mother had her talons set into the marble bed now, making indents in them in an Alligatorian sort of way. She spoke in a low voice.

—Never mind, we don't care how you sit or what jokes you have. We've heard about your jokes too. Don't use them on us, they are lame, mind yourself on the pathway of your miserable existence.

Immediately Brian had three jokes enter his mind, but he let them hold sway on the direction of the conversation.

—I know, my good lord and lady, the massive strength required to—

—And your unctuousness is out. We've heard tell of that and the primitive excitement that seems to have caused. I thought it was just lust, but it's more than that.

—Yes, my lord.

—And no jokes?

—Yes, my lady.

—Civil now, and that won't save you.

—Yes, my lord.

The two reptilians got uncomfortable with his smooth replies. In short bursts of conversation, Brian was at his best. He sat crossed legged, his Black sword stuck in the marble at his side. Brian dared not be away from it, within such proximity to the two saurians, soon to be his relatives, if lucky. That 'luck' extended only to Brian Miller, the parents considered the prospect a curse. He had to exercise extreme diplomacy to these parents, above all. His mind was re-routed, but the prospects were slow, some things he couldn't remember. Subtly, the larger star dragon spoke, in Universalian.

–It seems we are together. We are familiar with your history, one of the reasons for our, little disagreement earlier. I guess that's enough said on that. Had we known of our daughter's ravings over a simple human, we'd have put a stop to it, your Casper-look and white hair notwithstanding.

–You know I've met Death Incarnate?

–Such is the fate of all flesh, you just don't know it. Anyway, that doesn't impress me much. You came into the Universe and then you go. You've drunk star dragon blood and will live forever, I understand. That doesn't apply in a case like yours, you'll die by violence. That's just the start of your saurian transgressions. I don't have all day to go over them. Oh yes, I do have *all* day. I don't intend to waste it on you.

–I know I've done questionable things.

–Tomorrow we'll see you at the ceremony, and the Black Sword Leader has just arrived. Nothing more needs to be said.

The observance, uniting two saurians, Black weapons, and one human was a simplistic affair. The Prime Black Sword was officiating, and the whole thing lasted only five minutes. Special arrangements for the Black Sword Leader to come to Crocodilia were made by Larascena for the mating ceremony. The Black swords and other weapons, now betrothed, were all there, as were Clareina and Larascena. Brian longed for this day and he definitely looked it. He was now dressed entirely in a Black Alligatorian garment. He even had the skilled hatchets make black lines under and over his eyes, making them seem much, much larger. His long hair, white, they hid in a black hood-shoal of sorts. They thought he looked stately. Medeian and Demeterian just stood like boulders but didn't interfere. They were surprised by Brian's 'design' evidenced by their bagel mouths, looking at him.

Brian's own Black weapons stood by proudly. His newly-restored hatchet was getting married, too. Brian had a discussion with his hatchet, and knew he should let him be married, he'd have to choose a different hatchet on the Black World. His hatchet wouldn't hear of it, not in the least.

—My duty is to protect you, and even married, I can still do it. Besides, we're on Crocodilia now, you'd have to go back to the Black World, so I've saved you a trip?

—I'm really not worth your—

—Don't say what your worth. Your own sword will be married also, so don't give me the line.

—But if you think—

—And miss the wild adventures you seem to get yourself into? Don't deprive me.

With that, the marriage ceremonies commenced. The only question was this, for swords, knives, hatchets, saurians and the lone human:

—Is this your mate?

—It is.

—You are married.

Then, Brian was married to Clareina, the Lizardanian, and Larascena, the Warlord of Alligatoria. Similarly, Brian's Black sword, married to Larascena's sword. His hatchets were also hooked up, and a host of other weapons also 'bore the chain' of marriage. All was very simple. Brian had black rings, made of a titanium-like stuff comprising the Black weapons themselves. The rings were very precious, and he placed them over the marriage finger of each saurian. The saurians also placed Black-world rings he was to wear on the marriage finger (he removed the ones placed on his right hand, giving them back to Clare and Lara). Brian wore two rings. Presently, the _fun_ would begin.

SEVEN

WHICH SAURIAN WITCH WAS WHICH?

...I am waiting to live
Waiting to die
I wish I could ring in some bravery
It's a lousy fix
But the tree outside doesn't know
I watch it moving with the wind
In the late afternoon sun
There's nothing to declare here
Just a waiting
Each faces it alone
Oh, I was once young
Oh, I was once
Unbelievably young
—Charles Bukowski, poem So, Now?

As Told by Larascena's Black World Sword:

Of all, first, just this: *I was deceived.*

You won't think a Black World sword could be hoodwinked, but I was. There for the final debate, the Twins of Triton in the balance, on that Israeli Beach, and me a male, so consider *that* source. But so was everyone, except Littorian and Genotdelian. They weren't fooled at all, and the Lord of the Crocodilians wasn't even there! Let me tell the story, you be my judge. You'll remember the night I'm talking about, the end of two humans? I could 'hear' the unguarded thoughts of the teenagers. I could *see* everything, believe me, this: I was as haughty as a Black World sword can be, to my eventual shame.

Katrina put her guitar down that she was calibrating and looked soberly over her shoulder at Brian. His teeth were clenched. A little blood trickled from one corner of his mouth. The corners were cracked, Brian's eyes, slits. Katrina then looked over at Larascena who still stared at Brian, her light orange pupils seemed a pale flame. She looked like a mountain of muscle and power. The Warlord's dark green scales revealed not a hint of weakness.

And, for me, I was completely satisfied, and I had my guard down. And I don't like using the pun on myself, thing was, I deserve it. I mean, even when I was fighting Katrina's Black World sword, I didn't take her that seriously. The weapons and the person are one. In a case like this, the humans were sorta all over the base in regard to thinking. The girl didn't grip the darn thing right, not in touch with the mind. See, later, the humans were shown how to grip us. Oh, let me explain.

My world is Weapons, nothing else lives there. That's really all you need to know. So, anyhow, it doesn't matter which hand you use. I know how you guys grip swords here, you know, on Earth. You have all four fingers around the grip and your thumb wrapping around, right? Well, wrong if your graced (and I do mean *graced*, it's a privilege to hold a sword-at-combat from the Black World). There are six 'points' in all swords, that is, Point, Blade, Fuller, Guard, Grip, and Pommel. If you're going to get trained, there are more points than that (the Tang, the Wheel, the Ricasso, is just stuff you need to know in intense training, but not if you're going over the basics).

Sorry for my digression (no I'm not!).

You need to be *in-touch*, literally and figuratively, with the mind of the weapons, the Everlast-brain-itself, and that's knives, hatchets, any long bow, everything on my world). Not to betray other Brian Miller books, in this supposed-series, but the Black World is a *Weapon World*, there is nothing else. And never *should* be.

Let's take a human's hand, left or right, as a for-instance. Five digits (normally) right? You hold our Black World weapons like you are shooting a gun, not giving someone a fist, okay? Your index finger and ring finger are around the grip. Your thumb is going around to meet the index and ring fingers. But your middle finger and your pointing finger are up *touching* the mind of the weapon, see that? Our minds are located 'in the heart' of the weapon, saturating the upper level of the grip, guard and the bottom edge of the fuller. All of us can speak Universalian, too, duh, we can tell you where to touch us for maximum effect. Then the weapons can know your movements and speed you up to eviscerate the enemy. So, damn, she was just a human, she didn't even know, at least *I thought not*, how to grip us.

I've no excuse for my behavior. I've learned, though. I just thought fighting a creature like Larascena would be certain death for Katrina. Brian's gaze turned to the table with the scrolls—and the regular and Black World weapons. Upon the table were all kinds of swords, long, oddly shaped knives and several items that closely resembled hatchets with triple- and quadruple-sided blades. Most where from my world, some were 'plain' that is, 'the mindless ones,' just training weapons.

A word about Black World weapons, from my planet. Not shining silver and steel, such simple metals. The Black World plus-utra-titanium isn't the finest in the galaxy, it's the best in the Universe. On my world, we, the weapons, are completely <u>black</u>, to include our hilts. We are a kind of obsidian that sparkled and shone in the various artificial and natural lights. I heard the thoughts of the two human companions. *They're alive, you know. They call to us.*

What are alive?

Katrina got to her feet, in unison with Brian, instruments calibrated, pushing back-to-back until they rose. *Those weapons are alive. They grow on a planet of black, and they rise from the very soil and they live on sunlight like…like plants…or us. You know it? I know it, now. But Brian you've never used a sword, let alone that other stuff. And neither have I. Don't you think they laid it out just for you to take this crazy step? Oh, Brian, you're too tired, you haven't thought this out.*

Nowhere to retreat. No beach, after this one, to walk on.

I saw Brian break from the Russian and dashed directly for the table with the scrolls and weapons. Knowledge and death lay side-by-side. Could use of the one stop use of the other? It's chance Brian had to take, a gamble he'd soon make. Brian Miller was probably aware than every one of his moves was being witnessed. He was thinking about Principal Brodsky and the old man's wisdom.   Katrina   saw   that Brian's hand was on the table. In a few seconds, Larascena was next to the human. Brian burst out to the assemblage. =Larascena and her people advance their candidature for butchers of the human race! This does no honor to either the galactic community nor to Alligatoria or the Lizardanians, here nor on their home worlds! =You accuse without evidence. You use the language of Lizardania to distort the truth, to the ruin of the memory of your doomed civilization. You've chosen to defend a world whose natural course has run itself out.

Larascena was not in a mood to be further lectured. I would have told that miserable teenager to back off. Maybe I should have.

Brian moved his gloved hand in a flash. Reasonably, (I think *reasonably*) Larascena headed towards the table, too. Larascena instinctively countermoved.

The Warlord grabbed one of the long knives and thrust it in Brian's direction, all in one lightning quick motion. The blade buried itself to the hilt below the human's ribs on the right side, the knife was twisted expertly and withdrawn. Brian had grabbed a "peace scroll" off the table, not any weapons at all and then turned towards the Alligatorian. He got a look of unknowing, unsuspecting, curious. Then, Brian fell, as any human would. It looked like a grenade went off in his chest. Katrina ran across the sand and caught him in her arms. The Russian pushed under his inert body, cushioning the fall. The teenager pushed black hair from around Brian's eyes and forehead.

Larascena shrank back from the table. The understanding that she had probably killed one of the Presenters might have set her mind to the consequences. Maybe she only meant to defend herself from…a scroll?

=Brian, oh the gods, NO! Don't leave me!

The Russian ripped at her robes and stuffed a make-shift bandage into the gaping wound. No one moved to help. The aliens watching took in the meaning immediately. Brian was dying—as was Earth—for neither was there an antidote. The Twins were only the worst part of it. Humanity watched as their best, and last hope, left them for whatever fate awaited the foolish, innocent dead.

Katrina cringed at it all. For me, being a Black World sword with some experience, I was embarrassed and shaken. Larascena would never have taken such a killing-act unless provoked. And Brian did mean to provoke her, that much is true. I was so ashamed; once at just doing nothing, twice at the mere fact of this benighted sparring session. That song, "Cage" yes, that: It came to me, watching *Warrior Nun*; it all reminded me of Joan of Arc. See, I'd made a study of her. At that point, I didn't realize that I was going to see the Maid of Orleans in just weeks, outside a little month.

At the table, Katrina must have let her nascent Lizardanian training guide her. The Black swords and hatchets were actually calling to the human's mind. They attempted to instruct her.

Pick me, Katrina—I AM vengeance!
I, young human, pick me and I will slay your enemy!
Your cause is just, you will be invincible and know victory, lift me!
Face them with me—do and let them die!
Save your people with me—not that knife—use me young Russian!
Choose wisely—not her—avenge your world with me!
I can take the Alligatorian's life, select me, child, me!

Katrina's hands moved as with ancient knowing and experience. In seconds, Katrina placed a sword at her side, two of the hatchets in her belt and two knives. All the Black world weapons coached her.

Everything is (so, so) justified.

The Russian had lost her love, and she had visions of holding his lifeless body, like a silhouette, as the Twins ripped the Earth to pieces. That was her primary thought, I felt it strongly.

Anything. Everything. Justified.

The Russian yelled. Like something primal, the blades the only justice. Larascena stepped away from her comrades. Another Alligatorian came from their ship at a trot with an exceptionally long Black World sword, at least six feet in length, a huge blade, in a silver sheath. That was me, thank you, but I definitely listened with my unknowable hearing, feeling, all the events. I was black as pitch but gleamed like a apocalyptic storm. Yes, I'm proud of myself. I was slung across Larascena's back. She was donned for battle, now with a second-long knife like the one she used on Brian, and another strange looking device from the table—two three-bladed hatchets.

She raised her remaining arm to Larascena, with her Black World knife, raised to strike. Grabbed by the saurian with easy-ease.

*What's this? You're going to strike me with this? You ignorant simian sot. You don't even **know** how to hold the goddamn thing! I think this wrist bone is pretty suspect, so...*

And she broke it, easy as opening a soda can.

Snap and pop. Bone appeared, for all to see. Amid the inevitable human screams and nuisance blood, Larascena turned the hand 90 degrees, white bone sticking out, all expertly, and so serpentinely subtly. The saurian slapped the human, but not to unconsciousness. Her whole head was purply-crimson.

How easy it is to bang-up your skeleton, all it takes

is 15 pounds of pressure or so. I can move continents, but this, your mere bones? Post-pre-child's play! Without backing up an inch, Larascena met all seven of Katrina's planned swings with quick and determined counterblows, with her remaining hand. The teenager could scarcely believe the power of each move. Larascena then roared on her own, a deafening noise. =This will hurt. 'Course, you won't live to feel the pain. A lesson from Lizardania ripped into Kat's mind. She deflected a heavy left and downward thrust from the Alligatorian. Neither of them could get traction in the sand. That's a problem for me, a Black World sword, just something I need to contend with. If my handler is sliding back, that affects me, too.

Larascena steadied herself quickly and sent another blow, this time with her knife at the girl's unguarded side. Katrina's right shoulder ripped, down to upper arm, through cape, flesh, down to the bone. The pain was a horror, and believe me, I know what a Black World knife can produce. Katrina's ferocious attacker, a mouth full of huge, six-inch teeth snapped. Now Larascena whirled her sword around faster than any human can (even) move. The blow was not clumsily aimed. With inhuman agility, the Alligatorian caught the teenager through the left side of the midriff, slashing deeply. The girl fell to one knee and knew instantly that the wound was very deep. Larascena again took advantage, striking her in the skull with her own head. Another blow from Larascena sent the Russian's Black World sword flying away. Interestingly, 'this' girl didn't call the damn thing back with her mind, and I internally laughed at the act. The girl's shoulder and torso, well, it was close to done. Like Brian. Like the Earth at the brutal hands of the Twins of Triton. I lamented it, personally, but I supported Larascena. No matter what.

The Warlord was too strong for Katrina. None of the aliens

made the slightest move. Many turned away, some in disgust. The Alligatorian, without remorse, brought down her sword yet again, clearly to split Katrina in halves. The girl's last effort raised her knife with a dexterity surprising to my opponent, shunting me into the sand! Talk about embarrassing, boy, I was.

Larascena roared again the same, deafening war cry. She spun and hit the Russian's still raised knife with awesome force. The Black World blade whipped away in a wide arc, close to the invisible barrier that marked the Presentation grounds.

Larascena gathered up Katrina's hair, jerking her neck down. She lifted the spent human from the sand with ease, to decapitate her.

Before Larascena could strike Katrina's neck, the Alligatorian was hit from her right by a human missile, Brian on top of her. This very much surprised me. The brilliance from the crack of his sword on Larascena's descending blow lit up the night. I mean, I was really trying now. Larascena screeched with surprise, but not from pain. Brian, bleeding steadily but with a Black World knife in each hand, assumed the classic stance of a Lizardanian-at-combat.

Good show, my boy, I reluctantly thought. *Too bad it's all for nothing.*

Katrina's pride swelled she pushed Death Incarnate away, watching with wide eyes. Brian chose to spend himself at the end on that forlorn Russian. Larascena got angrily up. She threw sand behind her in frustration. The Lizardanians were shocked that Kat's dying defender had become master of one technique. Brian was determined that his death should be costly to Larascena. He knew that aiming a Black World blade up and along the scale line counted. Katrina knew it, too. But the doing was something again. Head-on thrusts to the impenetrable scales were useless, but beneath them, flesh clung to muscle and bone like any other mortal creature. Or so the humans thought, *then.*

Larascena came quickly with very heavy blows. Brian parried these, but he could not stop them. Each of the

Alligatorian's thrusts pushed Brian back into the shifting sand. He fought hard; as hard as an American can fight. Blows were exchanged with blinding rapidity. Brian's application of his newly mastered skills was proving something of a challenge to Larascena. But he was so badly wounded, Larascena unharmed and fresh. She did not understand the Lizardanian moves being applied against her. Larascena never came to blows with a Lizardanian. She did not know their art.

Brian's weapons helped him and gave him strength. In a moment, his right-hand sword was sent careening out of control toward a crowd of Parcharia. They moved, just in time, to avoid the weapon. Before Brian could even switch hands with his last sword, the hatchet of Larascena met the remaining blade with a deafening clang, like the ringing of a great bell. It knocked Brian over. Blade-first, it stuck out of the sand; the hilt waving back and forth like a sail in a storm. Neither of his Black World weapons could understand Brian, because his grip on them was incorrect. Brian sank down. Larascena saw this, too—but decided to finish him anyway. She raised her hatchet for the last time.

And that brought the fire out of Katrina, at least, I thought so. The last of her dormant strength, a Russian's strength on the brink.

The Russian roared. Insanely, she *fixed* her broken hand, which, later on, I knew was impossible.

Larascena turned in shock, half-expecting a Lizardanian to attempt to hold her from her spent victim. Instead she saw Katrina, only a wounded girl, again, racing towards the saurian. Such a yell could only mean she was now one with the Lizardanian art of war, as Brian had been—but certainly it was too late. *You still can't accept nature's judgments, foolish one!*

But Kat didn't answer. Her weapons would speak. Larascena took no alarm. Stupidly, I was now relaxed, thinking pathetically about the Russian.

Then, that dumb-ass Larascena threw me, her own Black World sword to the ground, shaking her great head. She was content with her knife and three-bladed hatchet. Well, I didn't know it then, but that was a stupid move.

At least there will be some sport in this.

Kat ran over the sand in a fury.

It was not a flight of blind fury.

This girl had learned the savage arts. Running the black blades under the Alligatorian's scales were the teenager's one, primitive thought. The creature before me yet suffered nothing, possessed her full strength, was rested and alert. The Warlord was overconfident. So was I. Nevertheless, I had high confidence that Larascena's remaining weapons could end the teenager.

Of a sudden, someone was waiving a Russian flag, just off the protective ellipse. The fellow was young, just a sympathetic teenager. That sent the Warlord off, big time. She left Katrina in the sand after an initial knife hit sent her sprawling, face down in the sand. The reptilian, speeding with inhuman ability, to the bearer.

The flag was flying on a bayonet at the end of a World War One rifle. Larascena appeared behind the teen and slapped him hard to the ground. The Alligatorian seized the rifle and broke it. However, the bayonet intrigued her. She smiled, thinking she knew just the place for it. Larascena smiled at the barely conscious young human.

=Mind if I borrow this? Not that I'm giving you much of a choice, really. Oh, you can have the gun back, all in a million pieces. Don't thank me.

Disappearing, racing to the Russian, she gripped Katrina with a vice-like bear hug.

=Too tight, 'little' Russian? You Slavs are so proud, and yet, you always go West, for your 'tiny tasties,'? Slavs is one-watch-letter away from 'Slave,' right? Wormwood, this. And as a slave, you don't have any 'consumer goods,' because you're shitty at making them. Guess you like Vodka too much. Chinese can copy, but everything you produce is rough, unrefined. All your sins, at money's whim? You foolish bitch. You go for 'Luke'-warm when you could go for *deathly cold*? You want to burn or freeze? The reason you can't fight, is that

~~you are all liars, all of you, East, West, Asians, whatever. The whole lot of you, enemies to anyone not-human. Hell, it's in your DNA to be opposed to anything really good!~~

~~Larascena shoved the bayonet, at her back, under the scalpel and out, in a rainbow of blood. Katrina's white robe turned even redder.~~

~~=See, Prissy? Didn't get your lung, need you to process this, before you die, you need to comprehend my thoughts, until you bleed out completely. Just wanted you to see the instrument of your death. And, you've seen it, 17 inches, almost the length of anyone filling me, that's the absolute minimum, mind. In two minutes you'll bleed-out completely, teenager-and-done, isn't that what you want? Die like Romeo or Juliet? Smile for the cameras, the blood makes you look like the Joker, I'm your Batman. And you are going to die, embrace death because a *certain saurian* despises your existence.~~

~~Noticing the blood at the point, Larascena ran a claw across it and serenely slurped. Of a notable sudden, the Warlord had a reaction and actually backed away from the ruined Katrina, leaving her crumpled like any piece of mischievous paper. She left the blade where it was, shocked. Then, she actually did the characteristic tilting of head and neck, a sincere act of surprise and profound confusion. I've long since recognized that from years of training on the Black World. A reigning conflagration subsumed the Warlord.~~

~~=What are you? Who are you? I can't believe it, you're...you're a...speak up, you witch-sometimes-bitch, WHAT THE HELL ARE YOU?!?!~~

~~Maybe because of the weird smile Katrina flashed, the Warlord tried a hatchet attack. The bayonet removed, the girl was once again on her feet. As a world of humanity watched together with many billions of aliens through their representatives' transmissions across the cosmos, the Alligatorian swung her hatchet with unfathomable force and speed...~~

~~...and missed.~~

~~Larascena killed==the empty air. Where she struck, the teenager wasn't there.~~

117

The human's hatchet buried itself in the back of the Alligatorian, between the scales from the left hip to the right, unleashing a torrent of dark, bluish blood, and ended up around the Warlord's neck.

The Alligatorian attempted to hit Katrina on both sides at once. Recalling her days in ballet, she blocked both blows, legs at 180 degrees, split to the sand, head arched back, the toes of the human's boots pointing upward to the stars. I was amazed at the move, myself. Then, she leapt over the saurian, legs to the night sky. Katrina was striking with her Black World knives, and hitting, too.

Larascena's cries of pain and anguish earthquaked the entire Israeli beach. On instinct, Katrina turned the weapon to maximum advantage, slashing below the Alligatorian's scales. With her remaining strength, finding yet another vulnerable line of scales along the back, she dug the weapon in until the blade was completely buried.

Not gods, nor giants...

Larascena lashed out with her knife, again slicing through the empty air. She swore at Katrina. Then, I was summoned back to the saurian. The girl leapt further back, the loose sands alternating as ally and hindrance.

Let me choose my words, if I haven't before. With a slash of Larascena's knife, the little and ring finger of Katrina's left hand went flying. Her arm, then, sliced to the elbow, the knife doing it's careful work, letting crimson gush. Not, as you can guess, to kill Katrina. Oh, not yet. No, I'm afraid this is letting that mean-ass-kick-butt side of Larascena emerge, just a bit. The Warlord wanted to play with her food.

This insolent human! Enough blood spilled to get all the suffering out of this innocent girl, Larascena would see to that. Katrina always presented herself as better than other humans. The mighty had fallen, grinded into hard sand, so hard was Katrina thrown to the inviting ground by saurian claws. Larascena, the Warlord of all Alligatoria, the strongest they had, keen on grinding Kat's fleeting energy. She'd gripped weapons, after all. And saurian weapons, that? From the Black World? Innocent of using them, Katrina's real ignorance offended the saurian so. Her 'innocence' could be discounted, the saurian playfully rationalized. A dragon, a *dragon star*, can (and does) justify anything and everything. Years of experience as a Black World sword convinced me.

Then, Larascena struck with Katrina very hard, to slice the girl in half. Katrina's Black sword was there. She placed it flat against the bloodied right side in a single, smooth motion, snug to the hip bone. I hit the Black World sword and sent Katrina head-over-heels.

Really, I didn't expect this. I thought she'd end up on the ground. *Clumsy me* landed awkwardly underneath the chest of Larascena, sorry to admit, as Larascena lost her balance in the yielding sand.

Katrina hit Larascena in the neck again with her hatchet. The saurian fell to the ground, grasping her twice-wounded throat. There was so much blood that the ground was squishing with it. Katrina struggled to get her sword into one of the several wounds on Larascena's broad chest. All there was left to do was shove, I was helpless, my naivete had me underneath the Warlord, in those last few seconds. I'm doubly-ashamed to tell it. If I could have foreseen the relevance of the Warlord's question! Littorian must have felt an all but irresistible calling to interfere, for he was now on his feet. There was an uproar among the Alligatorians who seemed about to come to the aid of their fallen comrade.

=And now you die, you damn ALLIGATOR—because you ruined my adopted country and killed my love!

=NO, Katrina!

It was Brian propping himself up with one hand.

=That's not what you're about! That's not why we're here! Don't kill, Kat! Show...them what...mercy looks like...since they've forgotten.

Brian's breath ran out. As a Black World sword, I was flabbergasted indeed when I heard calls for mercy.

One spark of decency, against this hopeless night, set against the certainty of a destroyed world. Katrina pulled back on the Black

~~World sword, dislodging it from an injury on Larascena's chest scales.~~

~~Katrina turned to the tight knot of Alligatorians, huddling in silence. Behind them another alien ship was breaking from deep space travel, shimmering as it materialized, slowing, hovering above the waves, closing on the scene of the carnage. The barrier parted for the new starship. It was a long craft with a large offset engine, like several others in the area. Brian saw it too, but he was too tired and close to death to appreciate its beauty.~~

~~Katrina paused long enough in front of the Alligatorians to throw her Black World sword at them. It landed in the squishy sand. The Russian sunk down beside Brian. Then Katrina looked up at the approaching Twins, glowing brighter and larger than ever. The contrails set out behind the Twins, like a nightmare. Those beacons of destruction were set on crushing a shiny jewel, the Earth. Katrina propped Brian up once again, running a hand through his black, wet hair. However, the *truth is telling*, even to me, a Black World sword.~~

~~Katrina *wasn't* Katrina!~~

EASY-EIGHT

PRE-SPARRING CRUELTIES

This struggle of the human female toward sex equality will end in a new sex order, with the female as superior.
—Nikola Tesla

Every gun that is made, every warship launched, every rocket fired signifies, in the final sense, a theft from those who hunger and are not fed, those who are cold and not clothed. This world in arms is not spending money alone. It is spending the sweat of its laborers, the genius of its scientists, the hopes of its children. This is not a way of life at all in any true sense. Under the cloud of threatening war, it is humanity hanging from a cross of iron.—Dwight David Eisenhower, 1961

Safely aboard *Tiperia*, Larascena, Warlord of Alligatoria, had an idea. She helped the Wysterian into a near-by corridor, linked by a great circle, out of the way of the other saurians.

–Now, allow me, Teresian, my Wysterian, to cure you?

Without waiting for a reply, Larascena sent her hand lightly on the bleeding left triceps, and magically healed it.

121

–Thank you, my Warlord. I'm slow to heal—but I know myself well. So do you.

–And what's that supposed to mean?

–You've felt my blood, with your healing, there, so you know.

–I know what?

–That I'm far superior, Ally-darling.

–Are you asking me or telling me? I think we'd better move up that sparring match…to right now, my little sub-darling-Wyiss?

The Wysterian smiled at Larascena with her seven-inch teeth. Larascena's only reached six inches. The Warlord was well aware of the strengthened power of Teresian's masseter extensions. In a serpentine way, she knew her weaknesses. Too bad her feigned healing didn't cover this.

–That would be delightful. Prepare to lose again, like you did on Earth with the Twins of Triton, right? I will crush you—but I will refrain from killing you, I've promised Brian Miller that much.

–To hell with your promises. *You're* going to lose. I'm older and stronger than you can guess, and I've never lost—except against you. Back there, disguised as Katrina, well, I didn't suspect I'd be fighting one of my own. I mean, who would? Very clever, making a deal with Katrina, getting her back to Moscow, mimicking her right along. That was my error. By your blood I *see* the way to defeat you. No weapons, right? I don't care for any. I'll lift you up and smash you on my iron knee. Let's do this!

Just then, Brian Miller and Katrina Chakiaya entered the room, got in between the two saurians. Brian clasped Larascena's abdomens, and felt his hand go a quarter-way through the puissant muscles—they felt like hardened titanium. Katrina, similarly, hadn't occasion to go for the abs of the Wysterian, but she was markedly impressed, as her hands went half-way into the mighty puffed-out structures, feeling like a platinum plate.

–Goodness, I've never felt something like this, wow! You're really strong!

–Maybe, maybe, my little companion Katrina, but excuse me

now, I've a sparring session with our equally *small* Warlord? Don't be my butler, be my companion, now please shift yourself away, yes?

–I'll make *you* small, smashing those school-girl abs in my claws. Get out of my way, Brian Miller Human! You knew we were going to have this out sometime—she defeated me on Earth, my only, *only* defeat. And by the way, I was ready to get up again, only other saurians held me back. Time for payback.

The female saurians, set to fight. The power had almost saturated the large room; both sets of muscles were on extreme-overdrive. A total of just less than 200 inches of biceps, triceps and brachialis, squeezed together. They *wanted* a brutal, but at the same time friendly, war. The reptilians' legs were an amazing sight—easily 300 inches on each, expanding for the anticipated destruction. The 'idea,' that this was a sparring match faded in the distance. Brian feared this would be like a Crocodilian-style melee. Death would visit someone. The humans were insightful to realize that; the combatants, not so much (nor did they care, in the slightest).

–Larascena, really, you're not recovered, this has got to wait.

–I'm recovered enough to beat the likes of *her*, a mere Wysterian. Move aside or I'll pick you up and pin you to the wall—to watch my un-waivered victory! Witness a Warlord work her over, *that bitch*!

Katrina decided on her own tact, parallel to Brian's dissuasion.

–Oh, come on Teresian, just think! We're on our way to the Black World? You, Larascena's sword? Against the wall, right there, yes you! You wouldn't let it get too bad for Larascena, if things go wrong (again!)?

–I'd have to interfere if things did go wrong. However, that could never happen. I've confidence in the Warlord's victory.

–If it did?

–I'd be there, don't worry.

–You see, Teresian? You, and I, *need* a Black sword and other weapons too. That's why you shouldn't fight her (though I know, in my heart, that you'd win). It'd be unfair *to you*.

The two saurians faced off. The reptilians sighed deeply. Both humans had hands covering (as best they could) the saurian's puissant, etched, and angry-veined midriffs.

They serpentinely thought about it.

–Can we just, well, *shake* on it?

Both humans joined in together. They knew it would be violent.

–*NO!!!*

The humans were well aware of the psychic war that could be constructed through the seemingly benign 'hand-togetherness.'

–It seems we are not permitted to engage in a harmless sparring match, Larascena, two saurian gods not permitted for a little play, by humans. I am depressed.

–And a double-shame though.

–Why's that?

–It would have been a glorious combat, you at my harsh, unyielding talons.

–It can still be. You'll be at my claws, teeth *and* talons!

–What's that, my little mistress?

–After the Black World. Then we'll, you know, we'll 'play' right, no one getting that hurt, I mean, 'hurt' for a saurian.

–Yes, after the Black World. Then, I'll pulverize you, in a good way. You'll remember me, though.

–Alright my little humans, you've won. Larascena and I won't spar now. Back off my abs, okay, Kat? You're also kinda on my boots a little?

–Alright Teresa.

The Wysterian picked up Katrina, then, in a good-natured way, as well as a star dragon can, setting the human lightly in her forearm. Then Teresian winked at Katrina. They left the room to Brian and Larascena, laughing together just like, well, your classic schoolgirls. Katrina was last seen to hug Teresian, then gone.

–You've won again over me, Brian. This is getting to be a routine. Pleased, my human?

–You please me; I just didn't want to give you up to her, an old Wysterian up against your godliness; there'd be nothing left as you smashed her all over the place. That'd set me poorly with Katrina, you know.

–Nothing can defeat me when *I'm ready.*

–And I'll just *forget* the Water World.

–Please do; I have.

–You're funny.

–No, *you*! See there? No, *you*!!! You're the one who is funny here, my little, and precious human!

Just then, Clareina came into the room, and scoffed, leaning on the entry door, arms folded.

–I'm afraid I'll have to stop your sparring match, Larascena.

–I've you against me too?

–And <u>us</u> too.

Korillia, Kerok, and Littorian then appeared too, coming up behind Clareina. Larascena then growled a little. Then she thought (reluctantly). The frown faded and she smiled broadly.

–I'll tell you what—

Of a sudden, Tiperia walked into the room, in human-form, arms folded, long blonde hair almost to the floor.

–They'll be no sparring sessions on my ship, if you please. That'd be like having a roaring cancer within my person! I'm crossing Space and Distance, formidable foes. I'm trying to get us halfway across the Universe to the Black World; I've no time to be bothered by two mighty saurians *warring* within me. Now, let's have some fun!

Pre-Fin

APPENDIX ONE

Post-Football-Pre-Game Analysis

Totally ironically (at least, to me) and to other saurians everywhere and everywhen, Larry King did an interview with Littorian, Lord of the Lizardanians, and his 'heir apparent' Soreidian, a couple of days after the epic football game. The Black World weapons set this up and King was very game. Soreidian was wearied, even though he had additional help from Lizardanians with his injuries. This was after the saurian football game, which kept them fighting for over three hours. In all sparring matches in saurian history, none had lasted so long. Both reptilians, drained beyond words, featured Littorian a little brighter, a little stronger, than Soreidian.

Table length in Larry's office was a big deal, at least to the Black World swords. First, the saurians could sit like Sphinxes, as they were used to. King didn't want to sit at any table other than his mahogany arrangement and with his favorite chair. The leaves were Australian Buloke wood, and still the reptilians were advised to take it gingerly, on the structure itself. They had to put four leaves in the table to expand it out. So, the counter was increased fourfold, just to accommodate their massive forms.

–On *Larry King Now*, a special, our soon-to-be-gone-to-the-stars-star-dragons take a break with us here to talk about their football game and answer a few of your questions. Littorian, the Lord of the Lizardanians, and his second, Soreidian, have joined me tonight. Good evening to you, my illustrious dragon-stars!

Soreidian was relaxed, sitting on a great Iranian rug which crisscrossed the carpet Littorian was seated on. Both Lizardanians were so tall, King had to look up to make eye contact, even with them sitting like a Sphinx.

–I'm glad to be here and what relaxing carpets you have. I'm just too exhausted to notice anything else, hit me with an asteroid just to wake me up, please. You've heard of foreshadowing; well, this is back-shadowing, that's something *dragon-esque* for you.

Littorian followed up, also at his ease.

–I like my carpet, too, Larry. Very good, you must have coordinated with Brian to provide such accommodations. Maybe I'll go to Iran, just before we leave, I'll put my companion on it. It's society that brings you these kinds of thoughts. Maybe that society will have Iranian rugs that I can bring home? This rug is so cool!

–Speaking of these Iranian rugs, which are predominately red, we are speaking together tonight just after the football game, and I've never seen more of a bloody fight in my life!

Soreidian just laughed.

–Gore cleaned up by the Black World weapons, too, so no human blood detectors, okay? And now you want to go to Iran, Littorian? Another delay in our departure. I guess the game was fun and I understand the Black World weapons. People'd be infesting that football field, who knows what they'd do. They paid out a lot of money for the 'inconvenience' of the game. I guess looking for sunken ships has some benefits. Was paying out all that money at capitalist rates a favor, Littorian? Probably didn't count. Tiperia won the day, I should have known that I was outmatched mentally.

–Don't beat yourself up over that (just leave
that to me), you just try to be Tiperia's lover, then you'd see.
Larry King had to provide some background.

–Tiperia is—

–A woman, a starship, and my lover. She's been that way for
eons. I can't get enough of her, and she is the only one for me. As
a starship she'd go anywhere, but it might take a day or two (or
three). She'll be overcoming that soon, almost moving place as fast
as thought (and maybe, just maybe, *beyond thought*). We went to
Lizardania, for instance, and also no time past here (Einstein was
almost right, but not when Tiperia is here!) and had a marvelous
session, and there was an Olympic size swimming pool that we filled
up with our—

–Littorian, I think that'll do. Tiperia outmatched me, during
the football game. That was unexpected (and I don't mean the
cheddar cheese, either). So let's not hear the details of this epic
deleteriousness, this is a family affair on social media, let's have a
little opposite-deference.

–Oh, yes, that's okay, because—

Soreidian just waved his hand.

–I really don't have the energy to break-up Tiperia and Littorian.
That would get the Universe out of order, and for this anarchist,
that's all the order I want. I'm not for including a circle around
anarchy. The circle means 'order,' or some shit, and I'm not taking
any orders from any source. Still, right now, I'm feeling very weak.
We aren't God Almighty, we're just 'gods' with a very, very small 'g'.
And I'm not too dumb to know that humans can defeat the dragon-
stars too, if they've got Black World weapons on them. I think going
up against Littorian over that football game, well, humbled me. I
can't believe I'm saying this but sparring matches don't have the level
of appeal in my mind, that they once did. I'm for leaving Earth, and
will, but for now, I've worked it all out of my system, sparring with
Littorian. I really respect him, but not his decisions, the physical
Littorian, as Tiperia says, 'You can't go no better.' Wish I'd known

that before the football game. I'll have to tell you, Larry, I was feeling so tired, I was thinking about asking for a respite. I didn't. You see, I knew my challenger asked for no quarter. I am so hopelessly ready to leave! I'm glad Littorian *will* be with me, I respect his prodigious strength.

–In the interests of time let's turn to questions from our audience. From Johnson City, Tennessee!

–I appreciate your saving the world, but didn't you endanger it all in the first place?

Littorian handled the question draconically.

–Yeah, in a word: You can't win them all, especially when teenagers are there. Best everyone learn that.

Larry responded.

–You mean human teenagers were a factor, that should give the adults some comfort. This next one is from Chicago, Illinois, yes, ma'am?

–I know that there are only 30 companions, but didn't Brian Miller make it so there are more? I understand there is a new ninth planet, replacing Pluto, with all kinds of dragons on it? Like 5,000 dragons? So, if you're thinking there is some kind of black hole at the edge of the solar system, the dragon-stars will take care of it?

–May I, Larry?

–Oh, please, Soreidian, you're play (so to post- football speak).

–Like Littorian said, you can't win them all. That's my humble-time, Larry.

–Uh-huh. What wisdom! Next call, from Biloxi, Mississippi, sir?

–Yeah, these Lizzies are as strong as Superman and, like, everyone that doesn't exist today! We are done for, aren't we, like they will attack us? I'm just trying to reach out.

–Either of you dragon-stars want to take on that insightful comment?

Soreidian just giggled.

–That would be true, if it wasn't completely false. My whole thing was to leave, with Littorian, with our companions. I value my safety more than I value your time, Larry. Thing is, about Superman, even the weakest saurian can separate him from his noggin, then you'd have a superhero without a head. That'd be boring, something that deters dragons.

–This one is from Lakeville, Minnesota, no less. Ma'am?

–Hello? Gosh, it's an honor to be talking to dragons, wow. Can they come to some of our colleges up here and give a talk?

Both saurians responded instantly.

–Really not!

–Why not?

The saurians were dumbfounded. Littorian drummed out.

–Ma'am, maybe you should read <u>Brian Miller & the Twins of Triton</u>, I think then you'd understand. I understand the publisher is defunct, too, a challenge for you. In a word, dragon's shouldn't be here.

–Then why is Brian Miller making sure that dragons will be here?

Littorian grumbled.

–Brian Miller is going with me, off this planet, out of this solar system, a long way away! That's whether he wants to, or not!

Larry intervened.

–I think that getting into a debate with Littorian will be like debating Donald Trump. It couldn't end well.

–Well, thanks a lot, Larry, and total yuck, and I mean bigly! Brian Miller is his own person, and I'd interview him, Larry, if you want to.

–I'd rather interview you two saurians. From Cleveland, Ohio, we have another question, please.

–Thanks, Larry, and good evening. I only heard the football game on the radio. I'm sure everyone wants to know why Littorian didn't just finish off Soreidian with a sparring match, either in the game or just after?

At that, Soreidian perked up.

–Could I answer that question, Larry?

–Sure thing.

–Thank you and just so. Mercy is all. If a saurian sees the soft white underbelly of a fellow reptilian, that is, when he is totally finished off, I think it's the higher sophistication of mercy that stays the hand of the victor. I think that mercy was shown to me by Littorian, and I'm not sure why. Really, I was defeated, and this is a remark that a dragon would roast a human-whole for saying, but it was true. At the end of the game I was a mess to saurian society. Littorian took everything and anything I had and still stood above me. It takes a lot of humility (but no humanity, yuck) to admit it, but Littorian does deserve the so-called throne of Lord of the Lizardanians, whatever that consists of.

–And me now?

–Remember that's with a war on compelling me to be Lord of the Lizardanians. The teenagers have wedged themselves in between that fight, and we are just on the end of peace. Brian Miller and Katrina Chakiaya have wretched our long fight with the Crocodilians.

Soreidian sighed.

–So I owe Brian and Kat again, this never ends!

–It will now. Thank you both for visiting, and not breaking anything. You can keep the Iranian rugs, I know that you are dragon stars and would take them anyway!

APPENDIX TWO

A SAURIAN VISITOR OF CARCOSA

–What else, Brian? You wanted an interview, right? Is that what your neighing was all about? About anarchy? Good that is something simply, and brief. We will go flying, hop on!

–Yes, my lord.

I waved at the Wysterian and Korillia and then flew off at bullet speed with Soreidian. I had no need to tell him of that sparring match, and put a mental-cover on it, I didn't need him prying around in my head.

We barely got level at 500 feet when Soreidian started, not knowing if I was taking notes or not.

–I do more good work just by accident than you do on purpose, all-the-day-long! I could pop your brain like a grape. Know that 'brain' and 'Brian' are very, very close in pronunciation (setting Universalian aside). I don't want to stop you from building your own scaffolding for your subsequent hanging. Know that, Brian Miller Human and beware!

Introducing Soreidian to the uninitiated isn't going to be that difficult. A top of the line primarily green Velociraptor, Goliath-Atlas gargantuan muscle-on-muscles, he really did stand above Littorian. He was extremely fast, too, the slow movements of your typical reptilian was just an old saurian wives tale. His sharp, reeking talons and claws could puncture anything like any diamond-pointed tack and could crush Smaug in one spirited tail swipe.

–I appreciate your willingness to be interviewed on anarchy, my lord Soreidian.

A little growl escape my wily 'patient' and then he sneered:

–Uh-huh. Make it short, Brian, lest you feel my talons skinning through your back-side-offal, .k?

Whenever Soreidian talked even with my swords in attendance with me, I felt shivers. My swords, at my request, were not on Lizardania now.

–My lord, I hope you are satisfied that your side won our little contest. You have a companion, the station in Florida is now in the hands of the humans, and Lizardania and Alligatoria have pledged to leave the Earth to its own interests. Surely that pleases you, right, my esteemed Lord Soreidian?

–You failed to mention that the Crocodilians have sent a peace delegation to Earth?

–Oh, that. Well I'm well out of it, sir.

–No, you are not. You aren't a very good liar.

–That is the truth, my lord, I'm no liar but I tend to exaggerate or under-cut, a bit. If I'd told you the Earth was flat, that would be the truth to me, 500 or 600 years ago, I'm just a human, after all. I don't intend to deceive you, my lord, so just forgive me.

–Another thing, Brian. Don't hit me with any 'mystery troupes' or any of that genre. And that's the one (only one!) thing we have in common, I hate the French guttural phrase 'genre.' No hard-balls either or I'll feed you yours! Stay calm, now, the waves are laughing.

–You mean 'lapping,' my lord?

–Is that a hardball?

I gulped, (so accordingly!)

–Obviously not, I've left my sword with some reason, so please you. Now, then, my lord: They say human conscientiousness, self-awareness, nature, as you know, created an aspect of nature, separate from itself, and we are entities that shouldn't exist and—

The creature laughed underneath of me.

–Who the hell have you been reading cuddled up in that Vermont jack-off-hide-a-way of yours? Nature 'created' an aspect of nature—you have no evidence of that, at all, that's pure bunkum! And humans 'shouldn't exist'? Hogwash and apple-sauce you are ten billion (appallingly weak) people and still growing, probing for food, poisoning, and global warming everything and everywhere, if it wasn't for the saurians, you'd run into a Malthus-Spencer-Pandorum-Soylent Green back-beat-bullshit-cookies scenario, you breed like roaches, until there is nothing left! And you, Brian, hugely spooging ropes on two of our saurian creatures, I'll never live that down, if they decide to reproduce through your weak, silver-back gorilla DNA. You humans defeat any chance of post-apocalyptic-welcome shit(storm) due to your sea-sick, ass-hurt incompetency! You would probably have some limited nuclear war, but that's solved now by the supreme magic of Teresian, giving you five planets, right? Talk about breeding your shitty species out into the virgin Universe, it's really lucky we have Anarchy going here, you aren't my responsibility. I can't believe a saurian would see some merit in this.

–And thank God one does, my lord. Only one. Is that anarchy? Now, people like to believe that they are special, that reality is reality, and that this is 'all for us,' and so time is a flat circle, and we'll do this and everything over, so anarchy under the Membrane Theory-

–All for you, human? Your shear pretense, your egotism outpaces even the saurians! You have the sentiment that outside of your space-time, from a fourth dimension, (hu)man, you don't have any idea what you're talking about. You have no facts: Time wouldn't exist, space-time flattened, eternity, time-spheres, time-circles, what idiot-shit! Your scientists are like infants who are penned up (and I like the analogy) not knowing whether the Big Bang is 'real' or not! All the human issues go back and forth, like a toddler would play with. How do you know that eternity doesn't have time? You don't know! Death created time just so it could kill, with what, with some meaning? Do you know that Death has any meaning? Oh well, probably you do, but no sane human does! And you are reborn? To the same life? Eternal-recurrence? How the hell do you know about that? What evidence? What utter, complete horseshit that all is! You have no evidence and that is what is philosophy, and I reject it all, and that's what an anarchist thinks about what isn't provable. You know the difference between old and young?

–Uh, less matters when you're old, my lord?

–Shocking. Tact is for people who aren't witty enough to be sarcastic, avoiding the sinister. Tiperia, the Starfinder, just as a for-instance, knows that 'any time' exists anywhere and she can go there with just thought (or nearly-thought, she's working on it) meaning that a 'second here' is a 'second' on Crocodilia, Alligatoria, and Lizardania and that 'the stars' are not history—to her! And don't think being surrounded by stars is staring at pointy white teeth, either. Don't think of a 'second' as a 'period' in time! Seconds are not 'time,' dummy! Oh, it's hopeless. And if you, Brian Miller Human get into any of that coprolalia submerged in you, I'll talon your lips off. Now, obviously you don't comprehend that 500 or 600 years ago the Earth was flat, and that was the truth, _then_! You are talking about ignorance when you are not talking to the Starfinder!

I spoke back, because I thought this was important.

–Seconds are a unit of time, right? But think about the will to power and, maybe, the superman, that this philosopher does—

–I'd mush, mash 'n' lash seven shades of shit out of the brain of any 'superman' like a glutenous slug! And I've got the 'will to power' for you, anon! It's Nietzsche, that's your watch-word for the bulk of this mega-shit-blast? I've got no dog in that calamity. Did you know he spent the last nine years of his life insane! He had a sexual disease, you see. Did you ever read _My Sister and I_? You should, with his sister fondling him. And maybe Nietzsche started World War One or maybe Two? Jung, Freud, and all the other philosophers

136

and other couch-potatoes just didn't have enough sex in their lives. None had great abs, like, for instance, me! That's as preposterous as someone that says 'What-does-what-in-the-where-now-then?' And, in Genesis, Old Testament, the sons of God got all the girls, in chapter 6? Oh, all of it is just a big-jack-off-zeitgeist-fantasy land; a red rag to a full-bull.

The dragon laughed and laughed. I thought that was good. I knew he knew a lot, but I had to re-phrase my questions about anarchy.

–Uh, yes, my lord. Now about anarchy, do you think that—

–So, you wanna know about anarchy, lil' Terran? Let me show you about anarchy!

With that, the saurian warped down, down, and I saw a little island, just like Johnson Atoll. Palms, or what looked like them, flowed on a beach breeze as we touched down. I slid off, with all the nimbleness I could, putting my hands behind my back, innocently looking on.

–This is anarchy!

At that, he stiffened his right arm, making a massive and staggeringly Herculean bulging bicep. It was mountainous and as big as my chest times two, really much larger, 55 or 60 strengthened inches, and almost that around. He 'put' the incredible structure at my up-turned face. I was shocked at the five feet of mega-ultra-muscle before me, a thundering pulsing power that, if pounded down, could earthquake whole nations. It was a massive, green-marble, veined ultra-mega-boulder at full-growth on his masterful arm.

–This is anarchy, this kind of mightiness, and I'm not using magic right now. This is in excess of what Littorian can 'produce.' I can control all matter, for instance, on this or any planet. I need nothing that I can't produce. The permanently alienated human I reject, I have the Tree of Life in this arm—I could destroy you and everything—or create your life forever-more! Anarchy is the stuff of Gods, mind you that! Of course, you will live forever, you have the dragon-elan in your soul, you have consumed the cream of paradise, you have dragon-star blood now. The only impediment left is you can die by violence. I also have another secret for your so-dumb-self: You will become a dragon, a saurian, too. Oh, sure, it will take time. That will be your fate, and I will have nothing to do with all of this. I'd leave you on Earth to die in, really, an instant, and that would be the end of you. Other saurians see it differently, and that's anarchy—I respect the difference, you see? I don't need any 'divine reward' I'll make my own. No one and no-thing can stop me. What do you think of this flex?

–That's the most amazing muscle I've ever seen, and it is gorgeous, my esteemed lord. I've never seen anything so etched and I'm widemouthed in awe; the peak I'd have to stand on tip-toe to reach, my gracious lord.

–Well trained, well trained. That genuine worship is a real nut-blast. Yes, you do know how to talk to us, your training on this is complete. Let me tell you something about human management and you'll see the connection to anarchy later. The "great" manager is the one who is not encumbered by the outside, one who is brutal to the core, uses people for what they are worth and then throws them away, one who takes the best and leaves the rest (so ignored and so alone). I hope you have learned at least that, from being with me, I am the opposite of Littorian.

He dropped the flex, but not his comment.

–The current Lord of the Lizardanians is not a micro-manager, you know, Brian. Every day I discover another confirmation of the correctness of my analysis. You humans take advantage where you can. That's how J.R.R. Tolkien did it, he scribbled on the back of one of the papers he was reading at his university: 'In a hole, in the ground, there lived a hobbit,' that which really made him known, he used his job and his class, and his contacts (with C.S. Lewis) to make his writing world-renown. As for Smaug, you've seen us grow in size, right? I could take that dumb dragon and squeeze his head in my forearm and biceps, and leave a big, vicious splat! As Ibsen said in <u>Enemy of the People</u>, we are strongest because we stand alone, well,

I'll tell you what 'alone' is, remember my exquisite arm! I could kill whole planets with that appendage!

Since Soreidian was using literature, now, I thought this might be the chance to jump in. There was no chance, of course, I'm dealing with a dragon-star!

–The laws are merely reflections of the whims of the ruling groups, or the groups with the power (money) at the time. Anarchy rules against this rubbish. The more surreal and unnatural the situation, the more neurotic humans become—at least the ones who are really thinking about what's happening. Strength is people but for the anarchist, his strength, my strength is all.

–Here is my ultra-philosophy for you, little Brian Miller Human. You for instance: no contacts, no introductions, no especial credentials, domestic-scene liabilities-abound, no money, really total weakness. You couldn't 'fake-out' the contacts, the people you really needed, and your stroke didn't help you. Of course, Littorian cured you of your stroke. What you do have my wily little human is skullduggery, a lubricious nature, avaricious tricks, illusions, bluff, innuendo, cryptic messages, salacious maneuvers, empty shows of force: You don't rely on guts, courage, risk and effrontery. Those latter are all illusions to those who don't really, really know how to live! You aren't impacted by that at all, you do know, or you will know, that life is really, really, and really again, important, just setting aside any religious crap you got (somewhere). Bravery, hero-courage, that's the shit, the crap, of those not knowing what life is or how to live it. That is one of your real weaknesses, your truly human weakness; you may be brave because you don't know the joy of this life. A saurian gave you that, the scales now fallen from your eyes, and now you are afraid to leave this life. Now you are scared of what is beyond this life, as any good saurian ought to be. I'm well-aware of the petty tricks and the feigned acquiescence, and I'm also aware of the splitting-activities and internal contradictions in just speaking with humans, oh fear not, my Terran.

He was going to crush me, I could feel it coming. Thank goodness it wasn't literally.

—Humans are all chalk-full of slogging, repulsive malignancy, all tale-bearing, overly insular, vacuous dolts, embarrassed over (so) nothing, sucking the raw life-blood out of all nations on your brown planet. What lickspittles and mental cripples all of you humans tend to be. If you didn't have dragon blood in you, you'd never see it, Brian, but now that it has been a month or two, maybe you can see it.

Soreidian went on, much to my chagrin.

—Oh, I know there are only three ways to 'get somewhere' in your human society: Know someone, be shit hot at a specialized activity—oh, well, there are only two—you have to have contacts, or you are sunk. Without the saurians, you are damned. You humans have a need for an entitlement that you really don't have. And I'm not talking about your particular damnation, Brian. You'll have to 'reckon' with that, and I understand the sin of plagiarism to be harsh, indeed!

After he spoke, Soreidian took off, his muscled, leathery wings just a private joy to behold. If Soreidian was Lara or maybe Clare, I'd have been all over them, fondling their wanton sinews to no end, at their extreme satisfaction and winking happiness. I perished my mind of that mischievous thought.

We flew along for a time, then the saurian needed to be praised again.

—So, you've some idea of my views of anarchy, right?

—Yes, my lord, I'll have to tell my companion he needs more time in the gym, working on his arms.

Soreidian couldn't help himself and giggled under my legs.

—Not that, Simian simpleton, I mean my words! I've never spoken so much before, and, if it weren't for your obsequiousness, (and I see why Larascena and Clareina like you—for now!) without that, I couldn't stand you for one more minute!

I decided to be bold right then.

—And so Rachel Dreadnought doesn't display a level of subservience, my lord?

At that, a growl issued forth from Soreidian's great head, and he looked back at me with a dragon's fierceness.

—Hey, watch it, human. Don't be so churlish, my napping-lackey. I'll collect your face out of my Brian-douche bag jar if you aren't careful. For instance, I could back-hand you with my razor-sharp tail for misbehavin'.

—Forgive me my lord.

—Forgiven. See? I can be civil. Now we will make a brief stop in Carcosa.

—Carcosa, my lord? I'm thinking of Ambrose Bierce and Robert W. Chambers and their discussion of—

—And I care why?

—My lord?

—Never mind. Or, as Lara would say, 'Never-you-mind?' Gives you something to think about as you're fapping away. I appreciate you're not doing that on my back, obviously I'd make you eat the result.

I'd forgotten about the cynical and scatological references that I mostly attributed to the late-Genotdelian.

—I'll tell Lara of your interest in the frequent scolds she likes to give me. That will be sure to titillate her so please you my voyeuristic and erogenous lord.

We flew over the island of Carcosa. Through the clouds, I could see that most of the city was underwater! It was, indeed, a metropolis, and it had a break-wall surrounding it, but that was long ago demolished by the ceaseless, pounding waves. There was nothing left and no visible life.

—My lord, how do you know this is Carcosa?

—And what do you think of me, my interviewing human?

—The saurian beneath me should be set-up on high so I could worship him adequately. You are a god-like creature of an unrivaled knowledge and mega-strength, the model and the extremity of supremacy to all saurians, and others not in that class, and that everywhere.

–Good. That is the name, and no other, notwithstanding your authors mentioned.

Carcosa, if that was the city's name, would be under the sea, before long. The city was a slow rift of absurd ruin. It had five fine towers, surrounding the city and three bridges, alas, almost submerged. The star dragon flew around the five-mile city, and the silence reached up, giving me the shivers. The sky above the lost city was of particular interest. We flew below the rising storm. Several mean-spirited clouds, pregnant with rain, threatened even more water on yesterday's metropolis. All the buildings and the cottages were ripped away, in all fashions. Only the bare structures remained. A castle stood above the town, in the central part, integrating with the Draconian, bird-shunned shadows, and this all looked pretty intact. Seeing the castle was like sighting a phantom, there was a mist all around. The patriarch of trees grew shorter as you approached the castle. The whimsical suns danced above the structure like a haunter in the darkening sky.

–And there we will find the King in Yellow. Now you can take off your mask.

–I'm already pretty invested with my facial appearance. My lord, I wear no mask.

–No mask? Yuck the human face is. And I'm not imitating Yoda, and I'll forgo smashing the teeth out of your head at not mentioning that shitty-dwarf. Thankfully, the King in Yellow is a dragon (of sorts), as you will soon see.

We flew right into the castle, into the great and arduous room, with the King in Yellow giving court. The vaporous clouds reigned through the room. The court was just dust now. You couldn't tell whether they were dragons or humans.

The King did look just a *little* dragon-esque, though. He had two arms, two legs, but the yellow mass of him just fell in, and the crown was bent down, you couldn't see his face. The wings behind him had all crumpled down and were dark brown. The skeleton was huge, I thought at least 14 or 15 feet tall. He had robes about him. The king had a mask, in his left hand. Whatever the king was, or could have been, was gone now. His figure, which reclined on his magnificent chair was smashed down through unknown years.

–Once this was a great city, and a fantastic land. Since we are on Lizardania, don't worry, only a week or two will pass on Earth. But here, in Carcosa, it is not so. There were dragons here and the Old Ones, too. I don't even know what the Old Ones looked like, those that dwelt in the land of Carcosa.

–Why are we here, my lord?

–This is a place I had forgotten through the eons. I didn't know it was in this condition. I thought you should see it, for your edification. The people of Carcosa lived under anarchy, and maybe this is what anarchy brings you. As you know, a dragon can never die, unless by violence, or because they just don't feel like going on. You don't realize this about companionship—it gives the star dragons a reason to live on. You aren't even conscious of the power you have on saurians, especially those that have you as companions.

–My lord, why are they 'yellow'?

–My color is?

–Er, it's largely green, my lord, (and your body is as fit as Atlas on 'roids, and just no homo).

–Uh-huh. So, you can conclude that dragon color here is yellow, duh.

–Please go on my lord.

–There really isn't that much left to tell. You saw the towers, outside, they rose to an extreme height and had an ellipse about the—hey, did you hear that?

Soreidian said it in a way that left me dumb and totally unprepared as I was forming a comprehensive picture of Lost Carcosa.

Of an (extreme) sudden, 50 temporal <u>beasts</u>, tall things, just appeared. They were dragons, without wings, and they looked kinda clunky and stiff.

Oh, they are just androids, and obviously on automatic. They probably didn't recognize me as a dragon, and don't worry I'll explain, my human.

I didn't bring my black sword, my lord or my Kerok-inspired pistols, either.

So?

I can't be much of a help to you, my esteemed sir.

Again, so? I can handle it, my frail human.

That's just it—Larascena and Clareina said I could <u>merge</u> with them. To become part of their defensive dynamic. Can't you do that, my lord?

Well, of course I can! Hell, that can be done. But there is nothing to fear here, I'll just explain everything.

For me, I wasn't so sure, as the mechanical dragons gathered around us.

Can we merge together, so we recognize each other's actions? I got your back 100, Soreidian!

Sure, just come into my mind, I'll guide you, this will be no problem at all. Geez, though, let me explain this to them.

Soreidian then prepared himself to be diplomatic (which was really a concession, if you knew him). He wasn't so much a chatterbox, but I hoped for the best.

—At Carcosa, I'm pleased to make your—

With that, the leading 'dragon-andy' just swatted Soreidian away, and he landed at the end of the massive hall. If anything surprised me then, it was the extreme power bursting out of these eight foot 'mechanical' dragons. Then, the andy-dragons turned to me!

I turned to the andies and politely said this.

—I'll be your mad-cap-baller-huckleberry! You andies aren't daisies at all!

Soreidian, for his part, just rose like a viper, very quickly. He was really mad.

—Maybe this will be something of a problem, my Brian. Quite

apparently, I'm going to have to try now. If you say I got swatted away, hereafter, I'll feed you your tail.

—My lord, I'm tail-less.

—No you're not. And your wives love your mini-tail, so don't lose it (on my account).

With that, in rapid-fire touch with Soreidian's mind, we 'had at' the mechanical-dragons. I was one with my reptilian now-friend, so in touch with his monstrous mind. Soreidian rose right up on his strengthened feet (and determinedly sharp talons). We then had mega-Kung-fu with the 50 dragon-andies. I wasn't 'fully' hit by any of my antagonists. I darted away, just like Katrina had taught me. And that was good for me, because punching through a cement wall wouldn't be a problem for any of the dragon-andies.

My mind was driven, and I saw the way this Lizardanian viewed the battle, I was looking through his eyes. He crushed his foes, and the level of computer and mechanical things was busy covering more and more of the floor. The center-mass-bulk-mechanicals just belted out of the dragon-andies by his monster fists, a staggering affair. I could tell he was insulted for getting ham-handed at the start of the conflict.

For me, I mostly kicked my hostiles and elbow-struck them in all the vital places thought to me by Soreidian. The star dragon was very, very harsh, seeking a crushing blow at each and every turn. He didn't concentrate on the head, but on the chiseled chest of the dragon-andies. My opponents were few, with Soreidian pasting and pasturing more and more androids, the reptilian taking on the majority.

Soreidian started by hitting the first one in the chest, muscle-manning right through and out the back of the belligerent entity, his back just exploded out, his mechanicals split apart, metal hitting and pinging off the floor. On the last one, Soreidian shouted out.

—No, no, Brian, save that one! Just let me question him. Come here, you dragon-ridiculous!

With that, the saurian went right by me, and ram-shackled the forlorn mechanism down on the ground, irrespective of his bolts and nuts sent flying, Soreidian's seven-inch claws around his iron neck. The throat was caving in, but slowly.

–Don't kick-off, baby-butt, until you tell me. Why did we receive such a welcome from the dragon city of Carcosa? I was getting all set to show the human around.

–You are invaders. Now take off your mask!

The Lizardanian was having none of this. I could actually feel his mega-authority just ripping out of Soreidian through his mighty claws. I forgot to tell the luckless-metal-dragon about who gripped him.

–And you are the last of the invaded, you metal beast! Didn't you know we came in friendship?

The churning metal voice rose.

–Look around you, everyone's dead, including the Yellow King, and I'm the last repairer of reputat—

In a pre-resultant roar, Soreidian smashed the throat with his right hand, and, with his left megaton fist, mushed the metal face on the floor. The splat sent computer-parts and nuts and bolts and other fancy-truck flying in a five-foot arch around his now-jelly-like cranium, smegma-izing him *entire*.

–Ah, I'm so done here, come on Brian! Hop on my back, I think you have a date with Kerok. I'm all done talking about anarchy as the last andy dragon is crushed by me. Isn't it ironic? Well, you probably don't see the irony, no post-worries. Now, I'm in a little huff about our botched Carcosa adventure, so it will be great to get rid of you.

APPENDIX THREE

EARTHSHINE SPECTACULAR

My angelic, so totally ripped, mega-serpent Clareina gazed over a particular and vast amount of grass in the Everglades. Asking Larascena if she'd 'loan' me for an evening the Warlord of Alligatoria nodded. Lara reminded me that she'd ask for *twice* an "evening liaison" on my return. I smiled at her, while Clare winked, and we flew off.

The dragoness turned East, rather quickly, and then gestured to a field, her wings folded in the twilight. The ocean, just over the tall grass a subdued blue. Clare considered thoughtfully.

—See those? Those fireflies? I've seen sights on other worlds, of course, but I haven't seen what this planet is capable of producing, so my jury is out. Clouds, I'd like to see them on display, alright? I'd like a companions' thought on all of this, not just my husband's feelings?

—Sure, Clare and stated quickly, your pleasure and my satisfaction are running neck and neck; and your neck looks vitally and majestically suck-ability!

—That's suck-able, hold your swift, horney horses until we leave, let's run with the tension. Remember, curiosity killed the cat, but satisfaction brought him back with a vein-ripe, raging, third forearm.

–Sorry, Clare, that was my angry, votive Clydesdale, down boy, nay, nay. I've got that beast under (some) control.

–I'm not sure you have. I think now we're talking turkey, maybe you can get your massive bowling balls off riding me, sounds like fun, I think my green posterior will be proteined-up, right?

I prepared to ride the dragoness again. Her muscled wings emerged from her back, immense sinews and her sleek scales moving slightly, giving me a cushioned seat. Being so close to her, I tried to see her as just giving me a ride; oh such, such impossibilities, as my hands manipulated here, there and everywhere.

–My lady, I'll keep my loins in check. If you are hungry, with the sea right there, we can go after a great white shark with fancy tartar sauce?

–I liked to be funny aroundClare, a failing I have (you probably don't think it's funny, you had to be there).

–I could break a great white shark's backbone like squishing a grape, and do you have some tartar sauce?

Just before we flew, Clare questioned me.

–I've a question for you, Brian Miller Human, just before we get started today?

–Go ahead, my lady.

–What are the ten books that have most influenced your thinking, my Brian?

–Oh, I couldn't 'take' just ten books, my lady; there are books by Richard Bach, like <u>Jonathan Livingston Seagull</u>, things by Jack London, Bernard Shaw, the Joan of Arc series (at least 50 books there), so many pamphlets, things on Oliver Cromwell, I've had a correspondence with Noam Chomsky, Chris Hedges and that Leftist literature, my anti-capitalism volumes, many hundreds of them and—

–Let me re-state my question. If I draconically took you away from the little Earth, and you could only bring ten books with you, what are they?

–Ten, well, I, I've just got to give you just ten names? I mean, there are so many books, by John Spargo, John Work, Olive Schreiner and—

–That's it my child! Oh, come now, I understand that your female Black Sword, who will be heartily employed, anon, is bringing all the work with you, tens of thousands of volumes, no, just your top ten, come on and give it to me.

–But there are books by Trotsky, like <u>My Life</u>, and Maurice Cornforth has a set of three books, and then <u>War Is A Racket</u>, by Major General Smedley Butler, and those three volumes that are under—

–Come, ten, now!

The Lizardanian was so Velociraptor-y right then, I just had to say whatever came to my mind. If there are books, like the classics: Dostoyevsky, Aristotle, Homer, Hugo, Orwell, Conrad, Poe, Lovecraft, Milton, well, they do have a place for me, to be sure. Then, I was thinking of 'things-dramatic.'

–Okay, your imperial majesty, not in any order of what's important, and we are just walking on the beach, and that reminds me of Poe's great novel, <u>The Narrative of Arthur Gordon Pym of Nantucket</u>, it was published in the summer of 1838, and this was Poe's only novel so—

–I'm waiting!

–Alright, my esteemed lady. I was just going to say that Jack London, Edgar Allan Poe and Robert E. Howard didn't make it past 40 years old but set that aside. I believe these books are: <u>War-What For?</u> by George R. Kirkpatrick; <u>Woman and Labor</u> by Olive Schreiner; <u>Bolshevism: The Enemy of Political and Industrial Democracy</u>, John Spargo; <u>Flying Serpents and Dragons: The Story of Mankind's Reptilian Past</u>, R.A. Boulay; <u>Notes for a Journal</u>, Maxim Litvinov; <u>The ABC of Anarchism</u>, Alexander Berkman; <u>The ABC of Communism</u>, by Nikolai Bukharin; <u>What's So and What Isn't</u>, by

John M. Work; <u>Rule by Secrecy</u>, Jim Marrs; <u>The Intelligent Woman's Guide To Socialism and Capitalism</u> by Bernard Shaw; <u>Merchants of Death</u>, by H.C. Engelbrecht and F.C. Hanighen and—

—Huh-huh, that's eleven, stop. Wow, such odd titles.

—I was going to mention <u>The Washing of the Spears</u>, by Donald R. Morris and <u>The Rebel</u> by Albert Camus, but I wanted to be in keeping with your top ten, and there is <u>Woman and Socialism</u> by August Bebel, but in keeping with—

—Tut, tut, I think I've heard enough titles. Your first one is most particular and peculiar. <u>War: What For?</u> What's that about?

—My lady, it's written in 1909 or 1910, four or five years before World War One, and it talks about the 99% having issues with the 1%, and socialism, and it's always been that way, I mean, the poor against the rich, a few humans always dominate the many. Thing is, when the 99% gets to govern then you get, well, I guess that never happens, but like that guy that wrote that thing on Rome, Edward Gibbon, said, "History is indeed little more than the register of the crimes, follies, and misfortunes of mankind."

—Doesn't that make you kinda cynical?

—What doesn't, my lady, if you are dealing with history? Unless you are 'outside of your mind' like the Nazis or the drunk Russians. Only then, at first, just at the first part of a revolution, you have a hopeful chance: The Germans made the Volkswagen and the autobahn, and the Russians equalized things, at the beginning between men and women, and there was, very briefly, 'all power to the soviets, or counsels,' but then Stalin came in. The anarchists tried to assassinate Lenin, and then, things started to go south. Those people couldn't handle power (well, they did, and the Holocaust and World War Two were just part of their answers) everything breaks down over time, you have Mussolini and Hitler and they all eventuate into dictatorship just to 'get things done.' Sometimes people have to be whipped, flogged and cajoled into action. If dragon stars were there, it could have been different.

—Gods with a small 'g,' hear that? I've got some books for you to read on Lizardania, and they aren't so 'cynical' believe me; they have the joy of dragon-star life inside them.

–Bring it on, my queen.

–First, this. My weapons, come and listen.

Clare whisked over my weapons, one sword, two knives and two hatchets and her own. Clare had one knife loaned out, so nine weapons pensively awaited their "order suggestions."

–I've a little game we can—

–Are we going to look the world-over for trolls, gnomes, spinners, maybe some meteors, transient luminous events, Clare, are we, *are we*?

–...play. Stand by, my excitable, garish knife. You'll have access to my incredible mind (and yes, I say so!) and via my telepathy, the things I need to see will be communicated to all, right? Pixies, halos, blue jets, right, and so much more. This time of the year is perfect for warping through clouds, anywhere around the world. And warp I will! Our weapons have their assignments. And we will see everything. *Time* is at essence, be off, go, shoo, shooed, and shooing!

The huge beast turned to me, smiling (I mean, *really* smiling).

–This will be fantastic for all the weapons, Brian Miller Human. All of them have the constant craving to be the first one back to report on my Bucket List. As though I, a dragon-star, should have anything like a "bucket list," that's for human's that'll die, eventually. 'Eventually' never comes for my people. Best that it doesn't. I wonder if <u>my</u> weapons will return first?

A knife reported earliest, one of mine.

–Clareina, my Lizardanian, oh! I have an aurora in Antarctica, you'll be pleased.

The massive serpent warped over to the South Pole in about three seconds, arriving like any Dragon-Whirling Dervish.

–You alright, my inattentive husband, didn't leave something behind in the sand, somewhere?

–Oh, sure, I didn't need my innards anyway, they are on a beach in Florida. Sure, I'm okay!

In shock, I observed the greens and blues, starlight all around, the sun almost set.

–I'll show you something.

Immediately, she flashed her muscled wings.

–What do you see?

–I do see the aurora down below, and to the left, it's so beautiful and majestic. As you know, me a natural bullshitter, it just comes with being a person, Clare. Can I have credit, I'm being self-criticizing.

–We are right in the greens you just saw, it's not green now, is it?

–No, my empress, it isn't.

–That's the thing: If you get too close to something, its value is suspended to you, things lose the luster, right? The birds 'singing' in the park; but what are they saying, really? Stay out of my territory, other birds! You'll see at the rainbow.

–The rainbow, my lady?

–Oh, sure, you'll see.

They watched the aurora, a very great one, for a few minutes, greens, and reds, purples, light blues.

–Charged particles from the sun, you see, strike atoms in the Earth's little canopy. That causes electrons in the atoms to move to a higher-energy level. When the electrons drop back into a lower energy state, they release photons of light. Now you know why you can't physically touch it.

Then she made a comment that shattered me.

–Hey, pretty good plan on getting with Katrina and Teresian for going back in time and establishing Wysteria as your new ninth planet, just as 'the saurians won the day,' in motivating you to leave Earth, right? I mean, can't have the third planet in a nuclear fireball (with respect to the Crocodilians, I mean) your tinkering around with our dragon-esque plans; you made a 'side arrangement' on the vulnerable Wysterian to use her vast amount of dragon-star-energy to return to the past and get her planet back. And that despite the zombie-affair that she screwed up with Kat? So, this new Wysterian planet couldn't permit a black hole or a comet, or whatever else from beating the shit out of your Earth, but for their own saurian welfare? Well and most cynically done. An accursed human genius must be responsible for this elaborate plan. I bet that wily Russian Katrina helped you there, say that isn't true and I'll demolish your mouth (and I might do that anyway)? And then, for insurance, you arranged with Turinian, the new Lord of the Crocodilians, to get into some kind of peace-deal here on Earth, too? You were enemies with him once? Even gooder, and that with almost 14,000 (or whatever) nuclear warheads in the world? You cut-short World War Three, right, with dragon-might? You couldn't blow yourselves up with dragons right 'next door' on their new world of Wysteria? You humans can take on gods, and deviousness alone will do, right Brian? And then, I bet, you planned to get more and more dragon-stars companioned off, a double insurance for you there, the dragons would prevent war because they'd 'feel' for their teenage humans. And you'd team up the entire Wysterian planet with them, 5,000 dragons, isn't that their population? War can't be the same, if everyone has a nuke, the rich and the poor will be blown to bits. And you'll do something about that, and you can't care what that is, even using your position and reptilian friends, right? Uh-huh and we are the monsters on Earth? Saurian's aren't the monsters, really. You know, you're the monster here!

–That's a lot to unpack, but let's just leave that suitcase packed to the full. This monster is married to you, my dear Clare. There is a black-washing cruel terrorism lurking within the human soul, can a dragon handle it or reject it?

–I'll do neither. Ah, Brian, again, we are not God Almighty, just your neighborhood gods, and that, with reason and you know how to defeat any dragon: With love in your heart. You see? I've got a good feeling about this!

Another weapon arrived, a knife from Clare's arsenal.

–Elves! I've got Elves over here, order number three, gang way, gang way, letta well-meaning knife through! And when you have an Elf, you have Sprites, too, so this is a double count for me. The location is Tornado Alley, I'll give you the GPS right now, the coordinates and then we can—

Clare was immediately gone to the exact site, in Oklahoma. A powerful Triple Sprite sequence was commencing, and even Clare was fascinated. The Sprite illuminated, just then, like a mangrove tree. She appeared way over the lightning just at the right time. Over the Sprites arena, Clare bellowed out, very dragonesquely:

!!!All Times Standing Still!!!

And just like, time and every-single-thing *did* stand still. Clare was instructive, gazing at the furtive clouds, and secretly excited that her magic had worked the first time, though she tried to be matter-of-course, in her speaking. It was so, just as I've said, so quiet just then, it was like a dream (only, it wasn't a dream when you were living it, really living it, only after, did you realize it was a dream.)

–Look at that huge jellyfish-cloud, three of them, discharging, you see? These are crawlers, trolls and tendrils climbing up the sprites? And look at that, a Green Ghost appears, just after that far left-hand sprite disappeared. I caught it in the middle of my Time Stand Still spell. That is 'Green emissions from excited Oxygen in Sprite Tops', so ghosts, right? It's all in keeping with the fantasy-nature of the whole thing. And of that, almost everything is here, the pixies, gnomes, hisses, whistlers, chorus, ball lighting, St. Elmo's fire, oh, we will see it all, my human. Look, there is a blue jet or a starter blue jet rising up? We are now looking, from this vantage, into the Mesosphere and Stratosphere. Very awesome, and I wonder how many people know about these events? You should see them on some other planets. I'll just let you soak it all in, enjoy!

I was in awe and so-many-shucks at the incredible event. I wished I could exchange a few words with this mini-god beneath me, and I just couldn't find the words. The tendrils went down to the lower atmosphere, and my camera and video recorder taped it all. I wondered if this wasn't "Stairway to Heaven," right in front of me. Clare pointed out with her huge, eagle eyes the intricate patterns of the event.

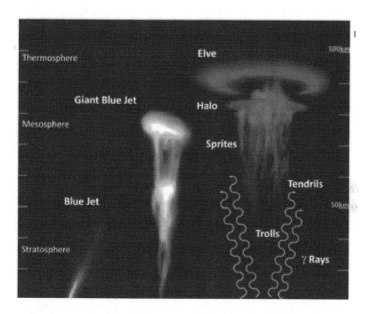

–It's all charged particles, negative and positive, nitrogen molecules in the atmosphere. A sprite is Stratospheric Perturbations mesospheric Resulting from Intense Thunderstorm Electrification. It gives off blue, red and all kinds of colors when you're away from it, just like a rainbow does, when the light hits it right, and there is the halo overhead, see? It's all oh-hum for yours truly, for sure, there was some power I was up against, and I didn't expect it's strength, but that's just because I'm young, and sorta inexperienced. That's just between me and you, my human husband, a dragon thinks they are the world (or more) in terms of power, sad, as this football game proved, that they are not. All the same, I sorted it, and then some. You weren't shocked, like physically, were you? Sometimes seeing things at a distance is better, and more loveable, that seeing them up close with all their flaws and imperfections. It's only with the heart that one can see clearly; what's essential is invisible to the eye. That's from <u>The Little Prince</u>, and I have respect for Antoine de Saint-Exupery. For the coup-de-scissors, let's go and find me a double or a triple rainbow, come on weapons, I'm telepathing to you and I'm waiting, let's go, let's go!

All the weapons chimed in at once, seeking to outdo their comrade rivals, thinking up all kinds of crazy stuff to say (or think!).

I have a huge rope of a rainbow, in Australia!

I have a double rain-bow-shot in Papua New Guinea!

I have a real nice double rain-Pterosaurs in Mozambique!

I have a triple-rain-facial-bow in Angola, Africa, off the coast, Atlantic ocean, here's the GPS and coordinates, it won't last long, it's peaking, peaking! And I have a Gustnado too, you know, a little mini-tornado, as an added bonus, pick me, ME!

—Angola, here I come, watch out world!

A huge, anti-wave washed up on the Benguela Beach, Angola, crashing out to sea, of course, created by Clare. It was a stormy day, that's for sure.

—Yup, there it is! There's the termination point. You know what's at the end of that rainbow out there in Western Angola?

—Just let me guess, like, a treasure chest?

—You got it. Sub-rats! You spoiled it for me, for shame!

Hey, look at that, Brian, there may be someplace over the rainbow, see?

—Where, my—?

Something happened, and I felt that there wasn't a dragon underneath me at all, then Clare returned. It only happened for a second.

The knife making the discovery showed up, one of Clare's. In fact, he was the only knife she had, loaning the other to Daenerys Targaryen.

—Oh, oh, I have the coordinates, all is prepared, right Clare?

—Yeah, yeah, don't give anything away, troublesome little knife, you're lucky I didn't lend you out, where is it?

Coordinates given in flashing telepathy, and then, in an equal-flash, Clare was only 50 feet off the ground, looking down.

–Ta-dah!

There, next to some Adansonia and baobab trees, was a massive chest right out of Treasure Island. Something occurred to me then.

–Oh, I get it. You located a sunken ship in the Atlantic Ocean, disappeared to go get that treasure chest and then reappeared under me, correct, my lady?

–An got a miscellaneous skeleton or two in the process, along with a case of flintlocks! That was a rare find, because the wood would have been washed away. It was preserved in a kinda vacuum. You should see them, against than Adansonia tree, that giant case of firearms? They're almost new. That was the real ta-dah, there! I haven't looked inside that chest, should be fun, yes? No?

–I think they should say at the end of the rainbow is a chest, if you are riding a dragon. Can we see it all, Clare?

Instantly, we hovered over the sight, and we dropped down. I went after the chest immediately, and I was fired on by a machine gun! At least ten outlaws surrounded the place, after seeing the dragon "make a deposit."

–Oh, my gosh, human pirates! Quick, the flintlocks, Brian, hurry, you're our only defense, help, I'm just a helpless lady, help, help! A staccato of flintlock-fire should be your answer, go get 'em, Brian Miller Human, save me!

Clare was feeling beyond-Superwoman right then, the bullets bouncing and ricocheting off her heavily muscled frame, disregarding the eldritch portent of the moment. The weapons thought this was a laughable situation, too. Still, she begged for help.

The Black World weapons, humorously, took the time to ping and glance slugs that would have ended me, too, so many where aimed for me. A few impacts I could survive, but I don't know about a whole slew of them. The guerrillas or pirates—or whoever they were—didn't approach the saurian but felt good about taking pot-shots at the both of us, aiming for my head, mostly. My good-natured hatchet (and one with the restored soul) helped me with the wardrobe-of-flintlocks, opening them lickety-split for ready use, in our Clare-designed Laurel and Hardy comedy routine. One hatchet then thought to me, just like Flounder in <u>Animal House</u>:

Oh, boy, is this great!

Inside where 12 Scottish Murdoch pistols and 12 muskets, all from around the 1770s. They'd been in the ocean for over 200 years, so I wasn't sure they'd even discharge. They must have invented some kind of vacuum-circumstance for them, because they were in great shape. What use flintlocks would be against today's rifle bullets tinkering around, was a mystery to me. I thought desperately.

Okay, pan, hammer, frizzen, frizzen spring, jaws from the flint (is the flint wet, or will it break off?), then cock the hammer back, ball, powder, rammer, full cock, aim, fire, I got this, but how do I, you know, load this son of a bitch anyway?

Then something occurred to me.

Yeah, the dragon is in control of this situation, she's cheapening me here, she can control any of these guys, why is she being so helpless right now? Well, never mind, I've got three or four of these tinker toys ready, come on, and aim low!

I started with a musket. A villain was firing at me about 30 yards away.

–Halt and put that rifle down, and it's my life, it never ends!

A hail of .30 caliber bullets was my answer. I fired and there was a hell of a boom. I hit the dude square in the chest.

"I hated to have to kill them all, but they had to be taught a lesson," ode to that old cartoon, Ralph Phillips. I think I actually said it, too.

Ah, those were the days. Why did they make only two Ralph Phillips' thingy-things?

The ball I fired was a .40 caliber and could put anyone down. I was proud of my accuracy. Then the pirate got up again. Not disabled, he picked up his AK-47 and fired. My Black World swords blocked every incoming bullet. Clare shooed them away, wanting, wishing to be hit! My other weapons were feeling bored. I grabbed both Murdock pistols and fired. Two chests, two pirates, perfect hits. And up they both rose, after a second or two.

–Clare, could use a little help!

–They have bullet-proof vests on you silly simian simpleton. I guess I have to do all the work myself, ho-hum. Just check this physicality-action-out and compare it to all the fights in *The Raid*, okay? Wow, I loved that series, good that you introduced me to that, watch this!

Then Clare went to work, waiving back all the weapons. She went to town on the ten pirates and what an extreme, violent, and, in parts, sexual site to see! Clare towered above them, goading them to take down a Lizardanian. The rifles were thrown down; the whole group approached the reptilian with knives-akimbo. I thought if guns don't work, what are knives going to do?

All the action took less than two minutes. Clare's massively cobblestoned abdominals actually pushed people aside, mushing them into trees, and this happened to a bunch of ruffians. The reptilian destroyed men's bodies like they were paper mâché, lifting them up, breaking their spines like the *Predator*, only worse, devouring men like ice cream on a very sunny day. One poor fellow got this arm ripped open, as the saurian gripping his fingers, sheering his hand down to elbow.

–I'm going to crack your femur bones into painful quarters, and then we will get started, right?

She broke the scofflaws backs, arms, legs, until all were moaning on the ground. A pirate ended up backwards, as she lifted him up with ease, then made the back of his head come together with his Achilles heel, enough said there, and it was a terrible sight to see, as his chest and stomach literally blew up in a huge field of guts, the saurian force was so great. Clare bulged out all her massive strength, flexing incredibly, just for me, her arms looked like Mount Olympus. One guy she just lightly picked up like an unrulily baby with a doll, and then shook him with ultra-extreme vigor until all his bones were literally broken. He was reduced to pinata-status, wrecked candy inside. When the suspended pirate hit "tube man" status, Clare, a mammoth, spouting Chernobyl of estrogen, the pirate all wobbly inside, she dismissively flicked him into an Adansonia tree, literally breaking him in half, scattering his fragmented bones. Another erstwhile fellow, witnessing, was just about to scream, and she taloned and clawed him to way-over-death, like a great, practically invisible, slicer out of the movie Cube. He didn't even know it was happening until way too late. That forlorn pirate just fell to the ground in bloody chunks. Another scofflaw, about to scream at the macabre scene, had his mouth open all the way. Clare maneuvered a left hand, right down his throat, emerging at the man's kippering, jiggling junk. The reptilian speared her fingers around this organ, and ripped a hole at the man's loins, then completely reversed his body, inside-outside! I've never seen a human being abused so, and I thought magic, maybe Black Magic, was involved. The others I won't say what happened to them, but one guy ended up a bloody tennis ball, crushed down with her iron hands, blood, viscera, organs, everything, matted together in her talented, but vicious claws. Then she literally swept her hands and claws clean of all the blood, in a frightening, and liberal, sheen. All the Black World weapons were stunned looking on, totally frightened. They'd cleaned up such reptilian violence before, but never had they actually seen the sausage being freshly made in a powerful saurian grip.

Then she leapt over to me then, yanking up, her 50-plus inch biceps around my neck, squeezing politely and subtly insistently, she was really wrapped around me, so-entirely. I was conflicted in my feelings, I didn't know whether to resist or gratefully concede to Clare's awesome, Lizardanian-consuming, crushing power. I saw right in her golden, silver and green eyes, mesmerized. So totally hers and she knew it, entirely. Mastered, just like a Queen's victim on any chessboard (anywhere) or anyone married for 30 years or more.

–And that's the reason why we can't have dragons running

around on Earth, right, my dear? Otherwise, you humans would just go all to molecular-pieces, see?

She really laughed and released me.

—We crave mystery because there is none really left, at least not physically speaking. But I'm not a mere Crocodilian, remember that, my kindness abounds.

Clare let the pirates suffer, but just a little while, and then cured them all with her astounding magic. Knowing they were profoundly defeated the simpering pirates left the treasure chest, scampering off, lowered heads like any just-fired butlers. Clare stretched, did an iron, pulsing muscle check all-around (which, despite her violence, I really liked). As the Lizardanian meticulously checked the mountainous layers of her left, cascading bicep, she looked at me warmly.

—At least I got a little bit of a work-out? See, I let them all live, aren't I great? Feel so totally free to be overly obsequious, prepare to worship me, right about now. Waiting. Now?

I was otherwise distracted by her muscle check, as she casually snapped the lock off the chest.

—Oh my God, look at the gold and silver!

—I guess it means something to you, doesn't it?

—Can I replace my kitty with it, my lady?

—You're low on whatever it is, what's it called, huh, money?

—J. Michael Brower came out with $100,000, I'd like to get it back, my queen. I'd like to give him $600,000?

—Oh, very well, very well! Consider it a gift from my empress-self. A knife was keen to the case, and made all the arrangements, like a great Black World weapon will and could.

—Thank you, and I'll be more attentive to you tonight, my dragon queen!

—That's the spirit. Breaking, crushing, snapping, and ruining those pesky pirates has given me a stunning need to be impaled myself with my husband's angry bludgeoner, and that for a long, long while, and yes, I'll flex mightily all that time for you, I know you worship my Clydesdale-like muscles, is that okay my sweetie-sweet?

I gulped appreciably.

–You know it's just like that, my lady!

I said this to the dragoness beneath me, flying back with her, just frustrated with how strongly angelic she seemed, I thought I was in an enlightened and superbly extreme dream.

–My goddess 'n' goodness just behold your esteemed elegance! I'm not trying to express in mere words what my emotions are right now; I really want you to feel what I'm saying to your unestimated grace. You're such a tremendous, dominant, stupendous sight to supremely see! How lucky I am to give pleasure to this immense, she-stallion-like angelic frame, this wonderful, fantastic gem, awesome, amazing and truly astonishing creature that is so high and powerfully above me, you're so lovely! You can be cruel and yet so instantly kind. I'm going up to tremendous, terrific heights with you, just touching you, my definition of glory-gloriousness-godhood! You are a woman, only more so!

And I really, really felt this way about this reptilian too. Everything about her ways, a muscled, enshrined being and it was definitely more than that. I didn't volunteer my evil thoughts, and she didn't insist. After my little speech, Clare noticeably shook, and responded, half-perplexed, half-laughing, yet all the while, leading up to something titillating. The Lizardanian looked quite vulnerable at this time, her mouth gawking.

–Geez-wow, well, I'm just going to cream myself right here, how dragon-embarrassing for me, but I guess I'll have to get used to this ubiquitous, white-rope-stream (ahem) of words, your being my husband, and all!

–and all, my lady?

–I haven't yet reproduced the ephemeral species (or two), but just give that some time (it is like I'm going to live forever-and-a-night, as you well know, or you ought to). Yes, we'll get to that. I will agree with Soreidian on this point, listening to you is a real nut, I mean, egg-blast!

–Oh, Clare, this has been so glorious, the pixies, the halos, sprites, blue jets and the clouds that looked like, well, just steps—

–You mean Lenticular clouds, with that lens-like appearance? We discovered those, with Black World weapon-help, in Harold's Cross, in Dublin, Ireland?

–It was great flying around it and then through it all, they were so still, it was superb!

–I'm glad you're enjoying it. Almost as good as those Altocumulus clouds over Mount Cook in New Zealand, right? It was fun flying underneath them, me inverted, with you on my pouting mega-ripped-stomach? I think you were looking at my bulbus, suckable abdominals and not the cloud formations overhead, I could tell because you were sucking them raw, slobbering down to my solid obliques? I'm not a suckling mink, but I'm trying to get along with my stallion-like husband. Hey, that's okay, my abdominals are a Ringling Brothers and Barnum and Bailey kinda Circus, just to make any human beg for more. It was all fun, yes, I'll concede that, rare for a dragon-star! I've seen many worlds' clouds, but that was particularly striking. Yeah, I've been hearing your radio, of late, and I do want to tell you something after I quote a song that Billie Eilish (and her brother, Finneas) sang:

As long as I'm here
No one can hurt you
Don't wanna lie here
But you can learn to
If I could change the way that you see yourself
You wouldn't wonder why you're here,
They don't deserve you.

And that's the main reason I favor you, Brian, and permitted you to evolve into a dragon, too. Humans don't deserve you, you should be a dragon, and, coming with me, that will be your inevitable fate. I do consider it an evolution, making Darwin proud, and you should think so. Or I'll make you think so, draconically. So there, you're with a star dragon now, have some needed respect. Now I'm so strong, mighty, so god-like (and always was) and it's like Billie Eilish said, *'Cause everybody wants something from me now And I don't wanna let 'em down.* Ah yes, that was fun. How do you feel?

—My esteemed lady, I feel fine. What clouds did we see again, Clare?

—Well there were those Lenticular clouds over those Transylvanian mountains, the Arcus, the night shining clouds called Noctilucents, the Fallstreak Holes, you know, the ones they we flew through, the wave clouds, or Fluctus clouds, called the Kelvin-Helmholtz, the cumulonimbus, and the mammatus clouds, you know, those 'mammary,' clouds that we saw over New York City, the cirrus, cumulonimbus and cumulus and then the rainbows, remember?

—Gee, you're as smart, as, as, a dragon!

—At least so, my darling!

Something was bothering me, something I had to confess.

—Clare I'm afraid Soreidian was right, and I don't see any way out of it, being a little human as you know I am. By the way, I see a parallel between the Carpenters and Ms. Eilish, and here's what I think: That girl better be careful, I know she's got parents involved in Hollywood, and that's what worries me. The things Soreidian said are mostly right. He said if you give humans anything, then they will want everything, experiencing a huge wealth they always and anyway want something else. You know what Samuel Gompers, the labor leader, thought. "We do want more, and when it becomes more, we shall still want more." I think humans can never get enough, and that just has to do with our limited life- circumstances we just can't control. Forgive us, is all I can think to say. Soreidian was right, in a lot of ways. I still want to make things right with him. You see? We still want just a little more.

Clare was dismissive.

—Don't ask the gods to forgive you; first, you humans should forgive yourselves. As life forms go, you're really not that bad. Ah,

Soreidian, he might have a change of heart now, post-football game. Plus, he didn't say all of that.

–Yes, but he *meant* to say it. And it would all be true, nevertheless. If you give the humans anything, they will need everything, too much for dragon-gods with a small 'g' to even handle. And Clare that's why it's better to be in the clouds, with you, rather than getting famous or listening to the silence, talking to celebrities, and stuff. Chances are they'd just want to get high, and we are, what, 62 miles up, so we—

–That's your 'Thermosphere' mind that, it's also known as the Karman line, remember!

–Yes, my highness, thermosphere, Karman line, the line for outer space. Of course, my serpentine wife, in conclusion, we are high above everyone, and it's just so lovely, as are you, Clare.

After, the swords, knives and hatchets arriving intermittently, we got to see all the clouds and everything on Clare's little bucket list. Clouds looking like 'steps' we most enjoyed, darting in and out, her picturesque dragon wings burning through them. In the end, Clare's weapons won out, referring far more "buckets" than my swords did. Lara showed up, just then, arriving alongside of us, looking splendid and mighty.

–Hey, you guys have a good time?

Clare answered.

–The best, lemme think it to you!

They had a happy telepathy. Lara cooed and looked longingly at me.

–Next time, it's on Alligatoria, I'll show you some extreme stuff, got it, dual-husband? I think Brian's reaching full-animal now, his venial piston, that exquisite truncheon, is indeed smokin' (hot), can we enjoy it later, our magic can make it so gargantuan!   I announced gamely.

–Yes, my dual wife, I love you completely, *inside and out*!

Lara dithered in the air, her iron wings wriggling, stalling.

–What was that, human?

165

–I said I love you inside and out, and I'll stake my life on it, anytime you want. That equally applies to Clare, too!

–Did you hear Clare? He loves us <u>inside and out</u>?

Clare murmured.

–I did hear, my Lara. Maybe he needs a *lesson* on what he's *really* talking about?

–Yeah, hey, good idea. I think that little hillock below us will be a great place for a lesson, the one with those trees on it?

They warped down to the little hill, the setting sun, fantastic rays jetting out, warming them.

–Only someone with mighty-might can do what I've got planned. Your weapons are going to participate in our little edification of today's human-husband. Very well, and then some. Brian Miller's weapons come here; hey, where yawl going?

They were following the conversation, just floating along at their extreme leisure class, some of the Black World knives were sleeping, the trip was so serine and pleasant. They were rudely awakened.

–Oh, hell to the no, no, NO!

Lara was angered.

–Tut-and-tut-again-big-league-sword-girl! You will come to order, and that promptly!

The sword whisked away, despite Lara's reaching out to her.

–Wow, you are special! That still that won't save you, my little Black World sword, remember that time on the Water World? You will comply and serve me now!

I was aghast, I didn't know what was happening, and I should have.

–What is going on here, Clare, what's the big deal?

–Your statement was.

–Was what?

–A big deal, human.

–Why's that, my esteemed lady?

–Outside and inside?

I was quiet, figuring out where my saurians were going. Lara whirled around like a ninja, and did snatch one of my hatchets, the one with his soul restored. The hatchet squealed like any old pig pre-butchered.

–You! Hatchet, come here, make an autopsy out of me, pre-postmortem!

Lara was so imperious with her bulky-self, the weapon was still pensive and very frightened. Clare was put-out.

–Oh, me first, Lara, I suggested it!

–Nuh-uh, I'm first, I'm a Warlord, almost the strongest saurian ever known, have some deference, Clare!

–No, no, not me I couldn't—

–You will, come here you singularity sprizzler!

–No, no!

My sword intervened.

–I'll do it, please release that hatchet Larascena. I'll do it, just like a human autopsy, right? Dragon-star wanting to prove something so uncivil. Okay, alright, just stand over next to the tree. Let's just get it over with, geez, I hope *you'll* appreciate this Brian.

Then, full-realization hit me, and I don't know why it hadn't before.

–You're not going to cut into her, right? I mean, even during the game with the saurians, no one ever came to blows, not even when Danillia knocked the French fries out of that officiating sword after the play was over and—

–I don't have time to hear this old bullshit. You know what to do, I've thought it all to you tardy sword, so just do it! Take a seat Brian, it's not like what you'd think, dumb-dummy!

Clare and Lara looked irately over at me, and I shut up. Clare giggled uncontrollably.

–Our human has discovered something, right Clare, and I didn't even have to brutally beat on him, either, bravo Brian!

The autopsy began and my mouth hit the floor, both bigly. Inside a saurian, it wasn't anything like the 'viscera' or 'organs' of a human, oh no. First, no blood 'gushed' fourth. Inside was just a great amount of silver, blues, a little red—really, it looked like a colorful rainbow inside. The blood was there, but it was 'disciplined' blood. And also, inside it was just muscles akimbo and all shining it deep, silver tone. Looking inside them, at the incredible majesty of raw muscle, you could see why number two and number one was out and out-cold, too. And it pulsed like, well, like it was sexually excited, to put it extremely mildly. I could identify some muscular organs, (many I didn't know, they were a dragon-mystery to me) massively gigantic lungs, sinuous, pulsing inter-abdominals, and a super, massive heart-bulging-muscle. Lara's gigantic pumping organ was silver and beating, no, thrusting vivaciously, hard as any steel. It was just as whopping as my overall chest. I thought it was "organ- esque strapping exquisiteness" the beating titanium, and nuclear weapon defying-ultra-pumper looked really proud to be on such display. The heartbeat reverberated much faster than it did for humans. I had to remember that this heart was eons old, and still looked vital, energetic, vigorous, vivacious and brutally <u>young</u>. Their tails were equally incredible, wholly (as in 'Holy') vein-ripped-muscle throughout, inside and outside, all massive, physical strength and lucid power.

–What do you think of this internal structure, my slack-jawed Brian? All of this, by the way, can take any weapons that humans care to play with, chemical, nuclear, conventional, anything, just the way my enstrengthened green scales can. I can't see the Justice League with these kinds of internal-muscle-dynamics, right Clare?

–Oh, you said it Lara. Now me, me, autopsy me!

And the reluctant Black World sword did so. Clare was as robust, spirited and dynamic on the inside as Lara was, with a brutal power known only to Lizardanians. Clare's arrangement was much the same as Lara's, only a little bit harder and more vigorous. Her heart was only half the size of Lara's, still huge.

–Come here Brian, don't be shy, touch my heart, feel my awesome, strapping power, step right up on tip-toe, come on.

The saurians drew close together and I managed to touch both brick-iron-pulsing-hearts. It was just like feeling very, very warm steel. Then, they actually flexed, and the amazing hearts beat a lot faster, like a mighty ship's engines at flank speed! Every muscle on the saurians was erect and pleni-potentiary-and-so-prudent right then and ultra-wow and just-them-awe-shucks-holy-shit-and-a-half-dollar!

–Goodness, these are very hot, just this side of scalding, <u>just</u> like my ladies.

Both responded, same time.

–Thank you, my child!

With the anti-autopsy thing rectified by magic alone, (it's good to be a dragon-star!) we were fully prepared for our evening 'meal.'

–And now, some magic I've been working on, in anticipation of becoming a dragon, some day. I hope you'll both have me, after I please you. Or if not, and I fail to give you pleasure, don't inquire about me you'll know where I'll be: I'll step off the Golden (ode to 'Billy' again). I've a gift for you, my dears, just call me Two Tongues, and you'll be 'known' by this super, muscular organ, that's for sure. And this isn't an exercise in <u>The Exorcist</u>, and I'm trying to be romantic, I'm sure you understand. I do like scary movies, but that's a personal flaw. Please, let's engage in our *ménage a trois*. I'm so glad you didn't see that porno-priest horror movie and let's just keep it that way.

I occasioned my queens over. Their scales and fins rose, and I approached them with a reverence, on our famous circular bed. The bed was magically brought from somewhere. I didn't know whose magic was responsible and didn't much care. The stars shined down. The reptilians didn't know what was going on, but they had their fun in mind. I hadn't disappointed them before, they lay prone, accelerating my potent mouth, until I was covered in their warm, glazing lifewater. I'm not going to talk about my massive pipe-n-piston, you know, my wrestling matches here with my saurians, teenager-sheen-and-ultra-goo-explosions. Disappointing in not discussing them, though: It's a glorious, so supreme, so mega-free feeling, my love for these dragonesses: *You couldn't go no better.* I've explained it elsewhere, <u>so have done</u>.

After many hours, causing my serpents to crest and peak more times than I can tell, covering me with gallons of saurian life-milk, I could feel them both really exhausted (in a great way). Completely satisfied (for now). I didn't even clean myself off; I was clean, clear, and suitably in heaven. Totally enough milked, be sure of that much.

–You know how you can tell you're in 'real love,' my glorious, super-enstrengthened dragonesses, you know what they say?

They murmured, together, in telepathy, both wrapped about our satin sheets in a saurian way.

Alright, my little human, what do they say?

–"Don't stop." See? That's real, dynamic love! My life has been totally reborn with you both. I'm so humbled and so blessed to be just a small part of your lives. We are all sentient beings, and if loving you is wrong, then wrong I'll be. And I don't care what <u>the world</u> says, so long as I can have you, over-and-over again. If anything, uh, untoward, were to happen to either of you, my life would be forfeit, and this life is all I know. You have my life, all of it, and more. That is why the young (and teenagers especially) know what it is to love a dragon-star, and, after that loving, wish death as a separation if they can't have them again and again, *ad infinitum.* You have total, absolute freedom in our marriage, and I encourage this, but I will be true to you in anything I do, before, during and after. I know all my secrets are safe with you and I'd sell my life, gratefully-enough, just set my life at any nappy's pin's fee, just to make you supremely happy. That's how I feel! It's okay to talk now. You don't have to genuflect to me, Lara, Clare?

I looked to right and left, after feeling a little ignored. Unfortunately (or fortunately, you be the judge), they were both soundly asleep. Either way, I saw something *shoved* over to me: My Water World diamond.

Couldn't go no better.

APPENDIX FOUR-AND-A-HALF

SAURIAN TEMPORARY LOVE

Larascena put her hands on Brian's ribs gingerly. Her tolerance towards the human was giving slowly back, she genuinely liked him. Larascena only half-wanted to squish him, now. And even that squashing, was retreating. She didn't like it, but it was happening anyway. The weapons rose to the deck. Larascena tried to hide it, but she smiled, reluctantly, gripping Brian.

–Fifty feet, coming up. Ready to jump aboard?

–Hey. Hold on a moment.

He struggled. She let him go.

Brian devolved to the sand. White. It was warm because of the suns. But not too hot. He smoothed it on his face. Soft. Like the days. Sunshine and ceiling unlimited.

Something black. He dug it out.

Larascena looked.

–What little ticketyboo do you have there? Why are you playing in the sand? Let's go.

–I think it is coal.

–Coal?

–Yes.

–Okay.

–Hey.

–Hey, what?

–Coal can be made into a diamond, with immense pressure, temperature and 1,000 years of time.

–Uh-huh.

–So?

–So!

–So.

–So. What?

–So can you do it?

–So can I do what?

–Well. Make this coal into a diamond.

Silence.

Larascena looked to the sand then out to the sea. She seemed to tense up her muscles, and sigh heavily. The Warlord walked away, maybe to jump aboard in another place.

–I said, can you? Or…or will you?

She hit him with a rapt silence. Brian stepped in front of her.

She stopped quizzically.

–Oh, Great Warlord of all Alligatoria! You are the most supreme, most magnificent, with more prestige than anyone; all knowing, all things crushing, crashing, and despairing before you and only you. The War Queen of the whole saurian race everywhere. All things yielding to you over time. Can you, oh mighty, supreme one, do this?

Enough to make men cry and women, positively swoon.

Now, Larascena, moved her head up a little, and considered.

Brian bowed, down to the ground, holding out the piece of medium, rock-size coal.

Larascena took it.

She crushed it. It took a few seconds. Turning her back to Brian, in secret, she held it up, looking at it. Larascena's eyes darted to

Brian. Brian was standing there, with his hands joined. He wanted, somehow, to provide her with the will power to mush out a diamond. Of course, he lacked the strength to do it.

–Hmmm.

She crushed it again. Larascena really, really smashed it, with unthinkable force, in one fist. A little mist arose. Then, it changed into smoke in her iron talons. Three pinky sized veins became enlarged on Larascena's gorging muscle. She strained until her biceps had biceps, they grew to huge mountains. A slight shadow could almost be seen on her scaled, green-blue veins.

She looked at it again. Now, she braced herself; a simple expression was in order.

–Ah, it was nothing, here you go.

A 32-carat diamond piece left into Brian's hand. Brian looked at it, completed mystified.

–Freakin' wow!

Larascena was amused. Brian's smile and brightness arrested her, and she felt moved.

–Yes, freaking wow. You ready to go up now?

–You are totally, totally, totally, amazing. The most super, supreme saurian anywhere!

–Oh, please. Yeah. Yeah. Hmmm. More. Please.

The two leaped on board the arc.

–I want to tell you something.

She put him down. The ship engine veered the arc away from the little island. She touched a button. FAST. The rising wind blew over them both.

–Huh? And what is that?

–I don't like Larascena. How about Lara, for short?

She soured.

–I don't like it.

–Then how about Scena?

—Double yuck. My own name you couldn't pronounce. Larascena is a good compromise.

—I don't think so, Lara.

—That grates on me. You wouldn't want me grated on, right?

—Well, no.

—Well. Call me Larascena.

She was a graceful creature. Somehow, you wanted to hold her, to keep her safe, to covert her. To worship her. A star dragon. The prize of the Alligatorians. The war champion of the race. But Larascena had female qualities. First, her need to protect the companion. A Lizardanian companion, but she still felt protective of Brian. It extended beyond what was necessary.

She had a wry smile. Brian liked to bring that out of her.

—I want something of you, Larascena.

—And that is?

—I want to kiss you.

—You want to do what?

—Kiss you.

—To kiss me?

—Yes. And, maybe, write a poem to you.

—Don't you think that's kind of weirded out? This is an alien, right? An alien flirting with me? This is something, er, erotic? And what's a poem?

—A poem is just a few words, you know. I've already made it up, here in my notebook.

Larascena just smiled blankly.

—I'm afraid my Universalian isn't measuring up.

—It's sort of a useless language, really. I think this is free verse.

Larascena was having difficulty understanding. Things saurians don't understand can cause some frustration.

Free verse? And a poem, what, written to me? What's my little human talking about today?

—May I, you know, read it to you? I have it, in my little notebook. You can have it, after I'm done.

–Is this traditional? I mean, to have the paper it's written on?

–Yes, it's traditional.

–Okay.

–It's called, "Larascena, My Lara." This is my people's way, of having romantic attachments.

–Wow. So you made up 'Lara' in advance of asking me. I'll have to watch you from now on.

Larascena said it all playfully.

–Cupid, he rules us all.

–Huh?

Larascena sat down, Sphinx like, for the second time, and pulled Brian down, too. She cocked her head to one side. She didn't like the shortening of her name, and she ground her tusk-like teeth noisily and her talons furrowed into the wood. But she listened. Brian proceeded.

Countless, countless, eons far-ago,

In an arc by the ocean,

An Alligatorian, a mighty warlord, there was, and you may know her

By the name of Larascena, the powerful saurian.

And this supreme princess, she dwelt on this Water World with no other thought

Than to be worshipped and to love only, and only me.

While she was older and older by far, we were still children of God,

In this arc by the ocean:

And we loved with a love two, three times the love of other creatures—

I and my Larascena, the saurian;

With a love that defied the sons and daughters of God, the angels above,

And they coveted the two of us: Her and me.

Now some will just love only to marry

In this arc by the ocean,
Others will tease and tarry, but that's not for me,
I have a blind love,
For Larascena and for me
But with my beautiful Larascena, the saurian;
Her people would come down, acting and reacting offended,
This was not my intent,
And they'll carry her off, to the stars, away from me,
And I'll never see her again; but they had not my consent
In this arc by the sea.

The sons and daughters of God, and the Alligatorians, all,
Went envying Larascena and me—
Yes, oh, yes. That's the reason, that's the reason,
For the question why?
And she came out of the arc, and they stole her away from me,
But this powerful dragon lives forever, and I've got to get her back,
And it will be me, me; and my Larascena, the saurian
I've got to get her back, back by the sea;

So I went to Alligatoria, and I spoke for her, and the angels sat in judgment
All were older than me—
Many were wiser and more elegant that little me—
But none of them, the angels in heaven, or the Alligatorians, or any saurian,
Anywhere, here, on the arc, way up in heaven above,
Nor Death Incarnate down under the ocean,
Can never, and ever, do anything about my love for this Alligatorian,
Of the beautiful Lara, my Lara
In this arc by the sea.

That is so,
and there is no,

no one to be between me, and the beautiful Larascena, the mighty saurian;

And we go back, back to the ocean, on the Water World,

And I will make her my bride, in defiance of the angels and the saurians,

Everywhere and everywhen.

And if we die, we die with the ocean in our ears, and endless love in our hearts.

Larascena, just sat there, with her mouth parted. She didn't know what to do. She didn't know if the poem was good, bad, or just—what? Could it be indifferent? Obviously, Brian wanted an emotional response. Larascena then struggled and set her great finned-head down. She didn't want to see Brian's eyes, eyes which looked expectantly to the saurian. What if she didn't give the reaction Brian wanted? Larascena set her claws into the deck, nervously. In her long life, no one had ever read her a poem before. Brian handed out the notebook paper, silently.

–That poem is, uh, sort of...er, epic, yes?

Brian, again, ceremoniously held the paper out to her. Timidly, Larascena took it, and put in into her belt compartment, with shaking talons. Her huge golden and silver orbs, lined with green, met his brown eyes, reluctantly.

–Are you hooked up?

–Am I what?

–I don't know if you're married.

–No. I'm not.

She was gearing up to something big. She crossed her talons and thought. The poem shook her up completely.

–You've had other Alligatorians before? You know, before this?

–Wow, I'm sort of offended, I guess; are you supposed to ask a lady this question?

–I have to kiss you. Geez, I have to. I can't help myself.

–Aren't you afraid I'll bite your head off?

Her mouth opened. Wide enough to capture three Brian heads.

Brian shrunk down. But Brian was somewhat thrilled to peer down her cavernous throat.

–Please be gentle.

She backed off. Utterly titillated. Larascena cooed.

–Gentler than I have to be, then.

–Well. I'm glad I told you.

Brian got up. He started walking around the arc. Brian was amazed that she finished it. The arc was covered with intricate details. She set up a table, with two chairs. The chairs, one big, one small sized, fixed into the deck, and looked like they'd never come out. She was into the minutia. One, two or three details overlooked all adds up to ugly.

–Now, hold on. This is something sexual, isn't it?

Brian bristled at that.

–Well. I'm kind of embarrassed to say. This isn't a reverse-Lolita situation, either. And like you say, it wouldn't work out.

–You let me be the judge of what won't work out.

–I'm sorry.

–Then you're looking to have sex with me?

The blatant way she said things alarmed Brian. But Littorian, Lord of the Lizardanians, told him different.

Be forward. Say what you want. Immediately. Alligatorians like forwardness.

–Gosh no. Well. Gosh no. And sex isn't a four letter word.

–Okay.

–Well yes. Well, some.

–Ah-ha.

–Look, I know you can kill me when you want to. Damn, I'd do it. That's. You know. Bestiality.

–Bestiality? I think it is more like pygmalionism, myself.

–Well, it's gross, now, see?

–Well, I dunno about that. And I'm my own alien. Counts out bestiality.

–Oh.

–And I see no advantage in killing one of my potentials, beast or alien.

–You don't have a steady boyfriend?

–A steady what?

–I'm trying to speak Universalian to you. It's kind of difficult.

–Say it again.

–Boyfriend?

–You mean friends that are boys?

–Geez. This is difficult. I don't know why I'm saying this. It's probably the way you look—you're an incredible example of super strength. I'm coming on to an alien, I'm ashamed.

–Anyone else around? Just us. And there is nothing the matter with you! I understand.

–But there are machines.

–Huh? They don't count.

–Okay.

–No. No boyfriends.

–Then it's okay to ask you. As an alien.

–Ah-ha! Protocol. I had a briefing at home. They said sex was a prime concern with humans.

–Oh. Sorry, then.

–Sex is a prime concern with us, too.

–I just don't want to violate anything.

–Violation? Right to it. Moving pretty fast, eh?

–No, I didn't mean that.

–What will satisfy you?

You'll satisfy me, he thought.

And then some, Larascena thought back.

–Thank God.

–God?

–Yes.

Now, she looked suspiciously at Brian.

–Do you know who is god to you?

This was a gawkward question.

–No. I don't.

–Perhaps, not at this time. I see. Now, about that kiss?

–Yes. And. And I want it now. I want it bad. And I want it all.

–Do you know what my breath is like?

–It's like burning roses. It's warm. Like the days on this planet.

–Wow. Well, yes it is. And how did you know that?

–There's a lot you don't know, but we don't have <u>time</u> for that!

And this made Larascena laugh. All her teeth exposed, above Brian. Her teeth were sharp, capable of ripping him into little morsels and tiny, tiny bits.

–Let's do it slow, at first. Mind if I French?

–If you what?

–Well. It's a French kiss. That means my tongue finds your tongue. It's kinda…intimate.

Larascena dismissed what she didn't understand.

–You afraid?

–A little. Yeah.

–Then let me lead, okay?

–Got ya.

They kissed. Brian was scared of the incisors, and the myriad of other teeth. He'd never kissed a reptilian before. Larascena was very passionate. She lifted Brian up bodily by the hips. Brian was four feet off the deck. Brian put his hands on her biceps. He felt those garden hose-size veins. Brian had a grip on her smooth, thermonuclear resisting scales. Incredibly, they tensed up, his hands on her peaks. Brian's hands bounced up, as she increased the might of her guns.

She gushed into his mouth. He tried to French kiss her. Her tongue was forked. It was like another alien itself. It poked his tongue. Then it wrapped and draped across it. A French kiss. The feeling, so near the Alligatorian's brain. It was a loving, velvety, electric charge. But it didn't hurt. He wanted more.

Divine. Exquisite.

Very good, I definitely like this, she thought-whispered.

–Littorian would have my head if I don't watch out for you.

–I don't think so.

–Well. Not so much.

–Alright. I do something dumb, then the deal to protect me is off.

–Alright.

The four suns, high in the sky—Brian was thinking about sunburn. For this world, night never came. Brian thought about the thin air.

–If I tried to run I'd be exhausted, yes?

–And that's something dumb. Don't.

–You need to sleep. I'll take the first watch. The sea looks calm right now.

Larascena grimaced and looked down at Brian.

–You need to sleep yourself.

– But you've been awake all this time.

–This is my saurian vulnerability.

–We'll be in need of your strength in the morning.

She smiled. Larascena addressed her sword.

–Sword, watch out—because morning never comes. Wake me if anything comes up.

Larascena's sword responded. It bowed with its blade down.

–Yes, ma'am.

Then the sword left them alone, going outside.

–I have my sword here, too. Believe me, I'm well protected.

She considered.

–Apparently. If you're feeling assured, and that's what I like, you can stay awake.

She went to bed. Brian tucked her in. He smiled.

Brian went outside, shutting the door. He looked at the swords.

–Now what kind of trouble can we get into, hmmm?

The waves calm, Brian's sword came back. Stuffed with fish. Brian's lighter lit up the spit.

After she slept for four or five hours, Larascena was on deck. Larascena was turned off. –How can you roast something that tastes so good?

–How can you eat something raw?

–Well. We both have questions.

–I'll tell you what.

Brian shoved the spit aside. She was curious. Brian's ideal state, in a star dragon.

–How about sushi, my friend?

–Sushi. Alright. How is that cooked?

–It isn't. Raw fish, cut up.

–Then why not just call it that?

–Sushi is shorter. It's a Japanese word. It's all in the preparation, you know.

–Well, let's see what happens. This time, you're in charge.

He examined the fish. He got out both of his knives.

We have to make this a Parisian haute cuisine as opposed to a blue plate special, Brian thought.

We understand. And you, Brian. Don't be a parvenu. Let us at it, thought the knives.

–I hope I get the recipe right.

She laughed, not even trying to help herself. Larascena put her talons on Brian, giggling.

Brian liked that. All her six-inch teeth magically showed up when she laughed. Her powerful upper and lower jaws had gargantuan shark's teeth, row upon row, backed up with fresh teeth, if one broke off. Brian never saw one break off. Brian was blinded by the prestige of the saurian's massive incisors. But it wasn't so intimidating. Her smile made you smile back.

Brian cut some up. He arranged it on a plate made by Larascena.

–This plate is also made by someone with skills. Someone I like.

–Right. Go on.

–We don't have any seasoning.

–Any what?

Larascena didn't understand the term. She was looking for more compliments.

–That's something to make it taste good.

–It'll taste good now. I'm starving. With the exception of you, it'll taste good.

–You propose to eat me?

–We'll save that for later. And I wouldn't eat without being eaten. Good manners, yes?

–Ah-ha. What now?

She consumed the plate. Brian was aware of her appetite.

–Good?

–It tastes a little plain.

–Hence the seasoning. That'd make it taste better. It's all in the preparation, right?

The work cleaning the fish was done by the hatchets and knives. The fish never stood a chance. They cut the fish to sushi portions in about five seconds. Brian made sure his hands were clear. Then Brian would prepare the sushi. He arranged it neatly on the plate, each individual piece having a separate place, giving the meal a finished look of elegance. Larascena ate it all. Last fish, Larascena acted laughably Spartan-like, having good manners. She slid the plate over.

–That's for you.

–Gee, thanks.

–Well? Better than losing an arm or a leg or anything else you have.

–I'd prefer the head. That way, I wouldn't feel it.

–Au contraire. Then, you'd feel a lot.

–Say what?

–You're being too high and mighty for the common ma'am.

–Say what?

–Again, later. You've really got your mind set on one thing. I feel cheapened.

Brian just stood there, quizzically. Now, say what?

Getting up, she nudged him as she went by. Not ready for it, he flew seven feet away on the deck. Hard.

–Ouch. Oh, I'm sorry, sorry! Here, let me help you up, oh, sorry, sorry!

She rushed to him. Larascena helped him up.

–Oh, it's nothing.

Brian felt his rib cage. Nothing was broken.

–I don't know my own strength, please forgive me! You've 206 bones, right? Any broken?

–Someone told me not to anger you. I should have listened. Nah, nothing's broken.

–I have to be delicate. I'd fix them, of course. Someone should have supported you, ahem.

She flippantly looked at Brian's sword. The sword stood at attention. It felt at a loss.

–Are you injured? I should have been there.

–It's okay. Larascena's just being a douc—er, is just being silly.

Brian's suddenly changed his mind at the coming insult. Larascena is a warlord, so be careful. Now, she felt awkward. Then, taking advantage, Brian nudged Larascena back. A steel wall would have been preferable. Brian staggered back. She barely noticed. Then she smiled slightly.

–And don't let that happen again, Larascena.

Larascena was not to be taken. Not in the slightest.

–When I nudge you next, you'll be off the deck in the water. Shouting your lungs out.

–Ah-ha. I was jesk jokin'.

–I think 60 fish a day will do. We'll <u>just</u> have to tighten our belts. Sword, see to it.

–I will, Warlord.

−Brian, sushi is preferred. And you're a good cook. You will see to it.

−I will, Warlord.

−Good. Well. Carry on. There it is. Chin-chin. And what knot. Now, don't twaddle around. And Brian: Do 175 pushups, just to see what I'm working with. And with one hand.

Larascena strode away along the deck, inspecting nothing. She pulled on a rope, tightly, rocking the whole arc. Satisfied, she roped it onto the straining handrail. Then, a little smile.

She entered the cabin. Brian was resting quietly. She didn't want to disturbed him. Still.

−Calm seas ahead. For the moment.

−Good. Now come here!

−Yes, sir.

Brian held the leaf blankets for her. It was soft. Brian wasn't sure how she did that. He'd never slept with someone like this. At least, not in the same bed.

Remember, boldness counts.

Larascena approached the bed.

−Remember who's in charge.

−I am.

−I am!

−I'll wrestle you for it.

She got in bed. She was really huge. Her weight alone could crush him. He could put a debit (or credit) card into each one of those ten stomach muscles. In between, they were that tight. Brian put a hand on her abs. Warm and steely. Hard as composite iron. There was no fat at all. The whole of her, total, heated metal. It would take two hands to get around those biceps. With lots of room left over. But with all that weight, the serpent in her, never went away. She was a boneless contortionist. Brian was amazed the way she could move and angle her muscular body.

—I can taste those burning roses now. You mind if I'm only in my birthday suit in bed?

—Not before we wrestle. I'm also wearing my birthday suit, too. That's all I've got!

Brian gulped.

—Well. I was just kidding about the wrestling. I like your birthday suit; it's <u>precrassny</u>!

—Thank you. But about the wrestling, I wasn't. What's precrassny?

—You're twenty feet long, I'm a shrimp compared to you. Precrassny is Russian for pretty.

—Twenty-five, all told. With the strength of 100 suns. And I see Katrina's influence, there.

—Now how do you know that about strength?

—Oh, I just made it up. Sounds exciting, though, right?

You're exciting.

—And I haven't lost a wrestling match in my life.

Larascena then tensed up a roaring, thundering muscle, her talons out-stretched. Thirty-five inches of venous rock, enormously extended. Brian touched the peak, way up. He couldn't move it, trying hard. She showed off her rigid abdominals. High, tight and fabulous.

Damn, thought he. He kissed it all. He salivated at the unbending granite of her midriff.

She laughed lightly.

Brian emerged from the cabin. Severely dizzy and tripping over himself, staggering around the deck, Brian wanted to engage in far-gone-versation with Larascena. His eyes caught her, but Larascena looked away. Larascena then peered at the sea.

—Do you love me?

The alien snapped back. She looked him up and down. Obviously, Larascena was already gone. Brian didn't even know how to behave after being dumped.

—We're almost there, this speed. I'll take care of the island myself. Then, to the craft. I'll fix it. Soon, we'll be off home.

–I'm talking to you.

I'm thinking to you, Lara!

She turned away. Brian (tried) to grab her arm. Unfeigned temper cropped up.

–Careful. And you're being nauseating. And you're not my little paramour anymore.

–Goddamnit, I'm speaking to you. You're not shit canning me, right?

–Don't swear. I thought Katrina taught you that. Katrina reminds me of your stupidity.

–I just don't give a shit shining.

–Just so. Tough talk for a 16-year-old.

She released herself with a little shove.

Brian went to Larascena. He got around her on deck.

–You again? You're being infuriating.

–Listen.

–No. No listening now. I can't stand the tedium. I can't scruple through your idiocy.

–You listen now.

–Who's in charge?

She flashed her giant teeth. Larascena's huge masseter muscle was particularly engorged. The Alligatorian can be menacing when aroused. Like right now.

–Do you want my life? Is that all you want?

Brian pushed her. He pushed her hard. She wasn't prepared, lurching backward, surprising the saurian.

–Then you take it.

–Someone else we know can take it. Oh, how lame, you are! Love, feeble, and weak—the guilt I feel, well, stronger. But you know something about that. And I hate all this repetitiveness.

Larascena was tired of him. The way any woman gets, given time. He was so impetuous, such an irritation! There was nothing "new" about him now, nothing. The strange feelings in her were strong, but she thrust them away. Nothing could stand that strength, not even love or guilt. Larascena hated conversations that went nowhere, like now. After all, she wasn't married to him; he wasn't the proverbial ball, shackle and tedious chain.

–I'm going to tell you something.

–Well, I'm going for a swim now. Relieve some tension. There's almost six quarts of blood in a human. So smashing you around the deck would entail lots of clean up. I don't want to strain our weapons. Boy, you're dumb and lousy in bed, oughta my way! You're beyond foolish.

Larascena's throaty voice had the ringing glitter of golden shavings.

–Goddamnit, you listen.

–If striking you would cure that cursing, I'd do it. Though I'd probably rip your face clean-off with my talons; say, do you remember me doing that to Katrina? Hell, I'll bet she does.

–I'm a human. I need love. I don't want your strength.

–Love? Not from me. And you know what saurians say about humans; with capitalism, one human shoots another; with communism they shoot themselves; with socialism, they shoot other humans; and with anarchism, the honest ones commit suicide. All of you humans, you're all fricking hopeless. So don't ask for such things from a saurian. And don't put your hands on me again. I don't like it, being felt up by your stinking fingers. I'll take your hand off, at the wrist, and throw it into space, hopefully hitting some of your home world's space junk. It's good we're getting off Earth, anyway—it's pollution-positive!

–I don't care about all that shit. I've never heard that crap, anyway—at least we're popular enough to have sayings about us. Do you love me? Will you, er, hummm, marry me?

–How you talk. Maybe I'll pop your mouth open and disgorge you of that vicious little tongue you've got, right? Littorian, I'm sure, can give you a new one.

–I'll ask eternally after I'm dead.

Larascena closed her mouth. Her eyes narrowed.

Silence.

–What are you up to? And you don't know Death.

–Do you Lara-god-damn-scena? Huh? Do you know Death?

–You shouldn't mess with something you don't know.

–Whatevs! And I do mess.

–Then you're a fool. And 'whatevs'? How incredibly tacky! Now you've got no respect from any saurian, for using such a silly, middle school phrase. You're sexually jacked! You dumb human! Don't make me your Xanthippe; shit, I'd never, what, <u>marry you</u>!?! So stupid!

She turned to the ocean. Hesitation. In her rant, the saurian hadn't meant what she said.

Larascena undid her belt and cast it aside.

Hooo, he's being aggravating, so annoying—I'd like to just crush the life out of him, then deal with him sharply after that!

The sea was rough. Clouds were moving in. Larascena brushed her thought aside.

–Don't do anything dumb, foolish or stupid. Okay?

–I'll be dead by the time you get back.

–Ah-ha.

Brian headed to the rigging on the arc. One piece of tree rope. Slim pieces of wood on the way up to the scaffolding. Not to be used. But part of Brian's design. He started climbing on the wet wood. The wind blew, white caps appeared on the ocean.

She paused. Indecision.

–What are you doing, human?

–I'm not your simpering page boy!

–What wonderful rubbish! You're going too high. Come down, you stupid human.

–I TOLD YOU NOT TO TALK LIKE THAT!

Brian was climbing higher and higher. Foot after foot. Larascena growled a little.

She thought to him.

Come down. Don't make me come up after you. I won't be kind.

Oh, I'll come down now. On your face!

The wind was now howling. Brian was at the top of the rigging.

–What are you doing, you silly, human dummy?

–Oh, that's it!

She was standing against the railing, huge arms crossed. She looked at the sea, shaking her giant head. In the distance, a storm brewed. Again. But of no matter to the Alligatorian.

Wow. These humans. What's Littorian see in them?

The 32-carat diamond piece hit the deck. It slowly rolled over to her black boots, shimmering in the fading suns.

Larascena blinked.

The strange feelings were now in charge. They smote her strength back as though it was nothing. And the poem stood before Larascena, on top of her now-pitiful strength, the piece of paper, just staring at her, with unseen, and human, brown eyes. Brian, already torn and shattered like any bombed-out window, let his feet slip and let his hands go.

She didn't know what any of it meant. He'd thrown the diamond down. Well, obviously.

Then, something occurred to Larascena.

Her arms then shook.

Her pride and vanity hid it from her. But she saw it. Always, she hid herself in those star dragon-induced sins. Now, in the lights of day, brought on by four suns, and a day that had no ending, Larascena could see it. Plainly.

Her heart skipped.

Losing. What does he mean to me? What does his life mean to me? Losing the love.

Losing the love of this teenager. The years accrued; but there was <u>nothing</u> absent him in life.

The temporary for-the-moment love. The poem, on the piece of notebook paper, destroyed by dragon fire. Larascena could see it before her, all consumed by saurian flames.

Now.

It was lost.

He fell. Back forward, into the waves. A brief life. He shut his eyes. It is over.

In her heart, something happened. Larascena then panicked. She panicked in a bad way.

The strange feelings had the saurian now, whipping her around like a Raggedy Ann doll. The thrashing in her heart crescendoed into a total frenzy, as it swelled up.

Then it busted.

Busted!

She wanted him back. She couldn't lose him.

Not temporarily now.

Not temporarily ever. She couldn't lose...

With inhuman speed, black boots sheared off in mid-stride, she slashed the floorboards with her heavy claws, literally tearing right through them. She leaped over the stern, towards Brian's falling body. The whole arc, propelled back by her powerful feet, bounced and rocked back 30 or 40 yards. The waves propelling the arc, blew back.

This world would stop moving. Time stand still! Time go backwards. She was so intent on not losing this human.

–Two swords, now!

Larascena was bursting over the side of the arc.

Two swords. An Alligatorian and a Lizardanian sword. Nothing could stand in their way. Nothing. They went instantly to her.

–What's the mission?! What's the mission?! The swords were almost beside themselves.

–Those waves. Set up a maelstrom. No water hits him. No water!

The swords flew over the side, ahead of her. They hit the waves with a physical and mental smack-down.

Brian never hit the waves. Maelstrom. The tide of water circulated downwards. Pulverized waves. Continuous, downwards, towards the bottom. The two swords swirled and sweltered. Brian's arms, set freely behind him, fell into the open jetty. Eyes closed.

Keep the waves going downwards! I have him!

Expertly, she cruised the waves. Brian's body was out of sight. She was fast.

His body came into view. Fastest. So fast, she caught up to him.

–Brian. Brian? Brian! Hear me!

Eyes closed.

–You're going to make this hard, you're going to be hard on me, right?

Afraid, Larascena dove at him. She had him on her back in one move. She lashed her tail around his waist.

–I gatchakid! Hang on, going up!

The tail steadied him. Then he draped across her back like so much unfolded laundry. Brian's hands touched the water, slightly.

Eyes still closed. No screams. No world. No thought. No one. No.

–Shit! Shit!

She swam up the twirling waves, her enormously powerful arms propelling her. Waves parted. She forced them back mentally. They moved like paper on a windy day. All muscles were engaged, functioning flawlessly. Larascena caught her rider in her arms, whipping back her tail, lashing it back with a strength that could split five masts.

The two swords, letting the maelstrom go, leaped aboard. One went into the cabin. She emerged with several leaf blankets. They sought after Brian, wishing for the huge Alligatorian to move aside.

–Let me see. Let me see. Let me-g-d-see!

They fought recklessly to observe the scene.

I couldn't allow that. Couldn't.

It was a day when an alien and an alien came together.

–Brian?

Brian came to. He was wrapped up-doubly in leaf blankets.

–Lara?

–Good. You can still function. You okay?

He touched her face. She didn't back away.

192

–Do you love me, Lara?

–Yes. Yes, Brian. Temporarily I love you. Anything. Okay?

–Temporarily. Yes, I think I can live with that.

–Yes...that!

–What isn't temporarily?

Silence. She looked at him steadily. So fragile. And this one. Yet, so innocent.

–You got me. I couldn't lose you. No. Now, hey, here's a thing you need to keep, right?

She dropped the 32-carat diamond into his hand. She closed his fist around it.

–From me to you, understand? Now, don't be a pain to me, eh? And yes, please take it!

–From you to me.

–That's right.

–I love you, Lara.

–Alright. Alright already. I temporarily love you back. Love? And I lectured you on that. And still you love! And I don't like you shortening my name! You know I can't stand that!

–Yes. Yes, Lara. Yes you can. You can stand that.

Larascena hesitated.

She looked into his eyes. Brian's eyes were wet with tears. So were Lara's. The Warlord blinked.

–Yes. Yes, I can stand that, and, and; well, I can live with that.

–You saved me.

–And I have you now.

The saurian hugged him.

–I will never lose you. Never. Not until I decide. Never (ever) lose you...

Ending Afterimage

Printed in the United States
by Baker & Taylor Publisher Services